ICARUS FLIES HOME

Debbie Burke

ICARUS FLIES HOME

To Rachel and Tim, with all of my heart, with a story that goes on forever

PRE-RELEASE REVIEWS for *Icarus Flies Home*

"A bravura performance!"

- Carol LaHines

Author of *Someday Everything Will All Make Sense*

"The author brings to light every aspect of a musician's life from fun to heartache. A great delight for any reader."

- Keith Gilchrist, Jazzman Music Marketing & Promotions

"Well-written...a story for our times."

- Sandra Marlowe, Singer/Performing Artist/Teacher

On *TASTY JAZZ JAMS FOR OUR TIMES*™ *Vol. 1*

"Inspiring artists, brilliant questions, overall awesome jazz read!"

"Insightful and inspiring read."

"Excellent picture of the state of jazz."

On GLISSANDO: *A Story of Love, Lust and Jazz*

"Dramatic. Arousing. Realistic. Unpredictable."

"Story pulls you in. Feels real. Nice work."

"Smoothly written and fast-moving."

"This jazzy read creates a sense of fun, mystery, and sensuality from the very beginning."

On *The Poconos in B Flat*

"A valuable and eye-opening history."

"An A-plus for *Poconos in B Flat*."

"This book does a great job giving us a long lost and important chapter in the history of jazz."

INTRO (Overture)

Short, empty glasses stood in puddles, their temporary owners no longer able to drive home.

"Round 'em up, ladies and gents. There are two open beds in the room down the hall and a pullout in the living room. It's been quite a night but Margret and I have hit the wall and need to say a fond good night. We met and exceeded our goal and we should all be proud!"

Beauregard Sonski-Abbott flashed a smile at his wife and took her hand. Three a.m. was certainly a respectable time for their CD release party to end, especially considering a celebration that included the legendary Stef Dalton, who had miraculously agreed to guest on one of the songs. And they all knew that Chanel, their guest vocalist, was on the cusp of extraordinary fame. Whether the CD charted or not, it would go down as one very remarkable night.

Though Bo was tired from his limbs to his core and his body cried out for sleep, his synapses were snapping. The sense of accomplishment after nearly a year's worth of hard work was palpable. He'd written all the music (except for one piece, where he collaborated with Stef Dalton). Then he met, head-on, the obstacles of having to coordinate the production online, hashing out every beat...that was only the beginning. Add in the studio time with his drummer Joey Fritz and Stef's favorite vocalist (and she might have been more to him), the beautiful Chanel; the Zoom calls to keep the project moving with a consistent voice; and managing and uploading the files to his producer uptown; the marketing, the press outreach, the podcasts, the launch date... Bo was weary just thinking about the enormity of it. Yet, it had all worked out. The level of gratification paired with the sheer mental and physical exhaustion had justified a crazy year of heaven and hell coming at him from all angles.

They had dug in deeply and completed the work that was needed before any of them – the four core musicians plus Stef and Shanny – knew it was possible. And when it was all said and done, they would finally drink from the chalice of success.

Nobody had any inkling that a certain influential Broadway producer would shoot an arrow into this bliss to destroy everything Bo and his cohorts had built.

CHAPTER 1

Little Dexie Abbott was the luckiest boy in South Carolina in 1927. He had a golden pass to the best honkytonk in town and was only eleven.

Dexie's dad, who in the trade was known as Jimbo Abbott (birth name James Washington Abbott), was in the house band at a club with no name. But everybody in town knew where it was – in the poorest (there was poor and there was dreadfully and hopelessly destitute) neighborhood, behind a splintered doorway on a dusty, unnamed side street. Folks just called it The Blue Door.

Jimbo was a fierce drummer. His sweat poured onto his drum kit night after night. He played with four other guys, sometimes even more. Up to ten musicians (or 12 very skinny ones) could fit onto the makeshift stage. Whenever Jimbo performed – only after dark and only for a sprinkling of pennies – he brought along his little man, Dexie.

Talent ran through the Abbott men. Dexie ached to be a drummer like his dad and showed signs of a killer technique that had yet to be nurtured. It was in there; Jimbo could hear it, and he could see the boy's determination.

Dexie loved to climb trees, not so much for the bragging rights on who could reach the highest branch but to find the strongest and straightest ones that could be whittled into the finest drumsticks money couldn't buy.

His frame was slight and fragile, but Little Dexie Abbott made up for his pint-sized body with a monstrous sound. He wailed on any surface he could find using whatever served as sticks, thrashing gleefully on the dirt floor at home, on his friend's porch or on tree trunks, mimicking his dad. With time he taught himself rhythms and the complicated interplay between the right and left hand. As he grew, his sound matured with a stronger appreciation of dynamics and time signatures.

Children were not allowed in places like The Blue Door but Jimbo viewed this as a guiding principle rather than a hard and fast rule. Like everything else in his life, he improvised as he hoisted Dexie up and through a back window. Once inside, Dexie knew his way around and scrambled down the unlit stairs into the kitchen, where he was admonished to stay put. His father knew the chef, who wouldn't mind the boy's presence. The makeshift club was in the basement, next door to the kitchen. One small, high window (too small for Dexie to have squeezed through) tossed a shaft of light into the club. It could be opened from the outside with great effort, and could then be held in place by an old tire.

Jimbo knew the little drummer earned more of an education in that kitchen than he would ever get in the one-room schoolhouse the next town over. "Now, boy, sit yourself in this corner here," he had cautioned Dexie.

"Don't you stray. You'll hear us just fine from here."
Then he gave the chef a wink.

The sounds that came out of that dark and smoky
room enthralled Dexie to his core. Vocalists had come
and gone; some were better than others; but they never
stuck around. The men who played with his dad, though,
had created a sound that Dexie thought could only exist
in his dreams. It was uneven and noisy and messy, and
yet the music was honest and raw, making this the only
place on earth he wanted to be.

The guys he'd heard on the family Victrola played
differently. The rhythms of ragtime were stiff,
regimented and predictable. They swung, sure, but not
like his pop's musician friends. And when it called for
scatting, they scatted differently than the voices pressed
into shellac. Dexie didn't know why, but when the
vocalists scatted on these records they always said "dit-
dat-dit" and "lada-ba-ba-dah." The guys in The Blue
Door did it differently. "Va-va-doe" they'd say, delaying
that last syllable as long as possible to exaggerate the
syncopation. That tension, that anticipation; it blew
Dexie's mind.

In the afternoons when he wasn't busy helping his
mother with her house-cleaning job (Daisy worked long
hours for a family on the other side of town), Dexie
scoured the neighborhood trash for materials to build
his own drum set. He was often joined by his cousin,
Beauregard Jefferson Abbott. Beau (*Bo Jay* for short)

was partial to the trumpet. He found a twisted-up bugle in somebody's trash (Dexie maintained he found it first, but already, the lines of demarcation over which boy would play what had already been drawn). With a little patience and delicacy, Dexie, the more mechanically adept of the two, was able to coax the valves into being functional. He handed the horn to Bo Jay with a sense of pride. "Now we gotta find me the makings of a good drum."

CHAPTER 2

Word got around about the Blue Door, and occasionally a curious white musician asked if it was okay to sit in. "These hepcats want so badly to swing with us," Dexie Abbott was later quoted as saying in the New York Daily Mirror. "It's not that they're bad, in fact, they're very qualified players. But there are so few opportunities for Negro men to play in good bands that my goal is to let these brothers really shine." The Jim Crow laws personified the endless discrimination, harassment and violence that black musicians encountered on a daily basis. The press tried to paint Abbott as a racist himself, but the jazz community knew better. He was speaking the truth. Only the brave would publicly agree.

Without even knowing it, Beauregard Sonski-Abbott was about to carry the family torch in a big way.

CHAPTER 3

You would never know by looking at him that Bo once suffered from a social phobia. When he met someone for the first time, he'd give off an incredible warmth. He was funny, a natural storyteller, easy to get to know and even easier to like. This was not the case in his grade school years.

By the time he was 12, Bo's lack of friends alarmed the school guidance counselor who gently suggested to his parents that he see a child therapist. His father was initially resistant but his mom pushed the issue, and it was a very good thing she did. Thanks to a technique called "soft-immersion counseling" Bo was able to manage his anxieties better. As an open-minded lad and being mature for his age, he had the intellect to consider her suggestions and try them out. When he started to make friends, scary as it was, he'd learned the tools to cope with his fears. He felt a huge boulder slowly roll off his back.

And then, there was the music. It stopped the shyness dead in its tracks, cracking open a whole new world for him. It had always been there, in the background, but Bo never paid much attention until the therapy opened his eyes and let him experience the world around him much more fully.

Bo had grown up to the sounds of his father playing trumpet, practicing for the occasional nightclub gig (which his mother wasn't crazy about, for a variety of reasons, not the least of which was the impression that *certain kinds of women* went for jazz). His father also got a few studio gigs backing up some of the minor-league instrumentalists of the day. Even when his dad had stopped playing and retreated into a full-time career in insurance sales, he had already made a lifetime impression on Bo. It was the father and son time spent together that made Bo aware of the far-off possibility of a life ensconced in music. He cherished all of the time spent with his dad but especially when music was part of it: scrubbing down the family Buick together with the radio blasting. His dad would point out rhythms, chord changes, harmonies and song structure. Bo paid attention and asked intelligent questions, and in this way received his early music education. Those were by far the strongest positive memories of his childhood.

When the oldies station was on, he'd listen for soul, blues and pop. Ray Charles was still getting lots of airplay in 1991 and whenever "Hit the Road, Jack" came on his dad turned the volume up. Bo's mom batted her eyes affectionately at Bo and in a campy stage whisper informed him that "he won't be comin' back no more, no more, no more, NO MORE!" It made sudsing the whitewalls less of a chore.

The next time Dumbo was on TV and Bo heard the song "Elephants on Parade" he bolted up. There was something familiar about it. He couldn't articulate it yet, but it was the walking bass line of "Hit the Road, Jack" echoed by the descending groove in the movie score he was now watching. The music elicited a limbic response: spooky and dangerous, yet it pulled on him.

A visit to his Gramma Ida when he was 13 marked the moment he knew his musical fate. He'd never paid attention to the black and white photos crookedly lining her dining room wall but something about them demanded a second look. Two bare-footed kids grinned at the camera. One of them crossed a pair of drumsticks in front of his face while the other held up a battered horn. "Who are those kids?" Bo asked his father. And that was when he learned he was descended from the famous Dexie Abbott.

When his father suggested Bo carry on the family line and join the school band, something clicked. *I'll take up the trumpet*, he thought to himself. *How hard can it be?* Bo already knew how to read music from impromptu lessons with his father; he obsessed over the lines and circles splattered over the dog-eared sheet music. Surprisingly, without being taught, Bo had an ear for composition and an innate sense of how chords went together.

Music had proven to be an emotional rescue from his self-imposed solitude and gradually brought him out of his shell. He looked forward more than ever to playing the horn like his dad and his grandfather Bo Jay.

It was disappointing to say the least when he found out there were already enough trumpet players in the band (in fact the whole band itself had the maximum number of students). Begrudgingly, he was shunted off to the orchestra class where he was assigned – not offered – the violin.

This was not in his plans and he feared it would attract the attention of the school bullies, which in turn had the risk of pushing him back into the timid boy he used to be. But he shook it off and accepted the ¾-size fiddle that his parents got him through the school rental program.

What he understood about technique came from his father: lip strength, stamina and breath control, none of which mattered in learning the violin. The other orchestra students already had at least a basic knowledge of their instruments. Bo had a lot of catching up to do before he ever came face to face with the conductor.

Because of a never-explained connection Bo's mother had to an Italian family at the other end of Brooklyn, an elderly patriarch who excelled in multiple instruments agreed to give Bo violin lessons for free. Bo climbed on the cross-borough bus at the painfully early time of seven a.m. every morning so he wouldn't miss the noontime church services with his family.

The only thing he knew about the old master was from overhearing his mother tell his father that he used to work for the "GE Television Theater." It was a program in the 1950s sponsored by General Electric which typically ran sappy stories portrayed by the popular actors of the time. It was accompanied with live music played by musicians whose faces were never shown and whose names failed to make it into the credits, only to be lumped together as "The GE Theater String Players."

The old man had two moods, cranky and annoyed. He withheld praise even when Bo made obvious and steady improvements in tone and technique. It was only due to his wife that Bo refused to give up. She stood in the doorway behind her crotchety husband and nodded appreciatively when Bo played, sometimes patting her heart, sometimes kissing her hand and putting it up to God. At least somebody was listening.

When the hour was up and Bo started to pack his violin, loosening the horsehair in the bow and wiping underneath the bridge where the rosin dust had collected, the elfin woman stepped inside the parlor and placed a wad of white napkins into Bo's jacket pocket.

The first time this happened, at his very first lesson, Bo was startled. He flashed a polite smile and thanked her as he put on his jacket to leave. He had no idea what she had hidden in his pocket.

When he stepped outside into the cold morning air, he reached into the folds of his jacket and drew out his parting gift. Wrapped in the soft, white squares sat six beautiful cookies, some made of meringue, some dipped in chocolate, some smelling faintly of rum.

This was the validation he'd been seeking, and he was certain it was a sign of friendship. Though the old man never so much as cracked a smile, Bo understood that the lessons gave his reluctant mentor a sense of purpose. Maybe he really even liked the boy.

Between the Beethoven and the Bach, though, the violin started to feel limiting. Bo longed to break free into more dynamic and exciting music. A twist of fate was about to occur that would set the course for a world he never thought he'd be given entry to.

He was about to turn the corner and walk straight into jazz.

CHAPTER 4

Bo did not hate the violin lessons. He only hated the long trek on an early bus to reach his mentor's home. He also wasn't fond of the jabs he got from the tough kids at school (there were some who ridiculed his choice of instrument as being feminine; as if the beautiful and healing world of music was sloped to one gender or the other). This didn't deter him. Music was a healer and a friend that was here to stay.

In his last year of junior high school, the orchestra had a sudden spike in violin players. He'd made it to first chair of the second violin section the year before, which was an amazing accomplishment, but he was drawn to the depth of the sound from the back of the room, from the two bass players. Surely with only two uprights supporting 27 other kids, they could use another bassist?

The orchestra teacher was skeptical. "You have to learn bass clef, and unless you have math in your DNA, it's going to be hard to make the switch just like *that*." He snapped his fingers.

Bo was determined to get to the back of the room. He told the teacher he'd study hard and begged to be given the chance. The teacher saw the spark and didn't want to be the one who discouraged a young man who was clearly infatuated with the bass. "Go ahead. But you better get up to speed fast," he warned.

Bo recalled what his upper-classmen friends had told him about handling such a big, heavy instrument. A multitude of symptoms plagued him: callouses, wrist snags and neck strain from peering up at the top of the instrument which towered over him. And now he would wear these afflictions like a badge of honor. He was finally a bassist!

Each class started with a full 20 minutes of theory before students were allowed to open their sheet music or touch their instruments. Bo had never even stood next to a bass until now. With its size and curves, it felt as though he were standing behind a powerful, wise woman. A sweet musty scent radiated off the varnish of the body which contrasted with the slightly acrid smell of the strings. The long neck pressed back into his left hand with surprising heft; he'd need to use more strength than he expected to support it. His right hand grasped the bow with a muscle memory that came from playing violin, and he could wiggle free the tip of his index finger and tap the strings. Just a dab, not a full-fledged pluck. Would he dare try? As the teacher droned on about the circle of fifths to the collective groan of the class, there was a knock on the door by another teacher and he was called out of the room.

This was Bo's shot. He couldn't wait a millisecond longer. Placing his still-growing paws on the fretboard, his heart pounding a crazy-dance under his royal blue school polo shirt, Bo intuited that the walking bass line, those dungeon-like downward steps he remembered from Disney, could be achieved with one finger. He pressed his left index finger down against one of the thick strings and continued to slide it further up the neck, plucking quietly with his other hand and, to his surprise, nailing it. The moment produced a brilliant flash of light flooding his cerebral cortex. He knew at that instant he was home.

What he didn't know was that it was the first step of the journey would eventually take him to one of the darkest places that humankind had ever been.

CHAPTER 5

Bo's music life had been good to him: finding three friends to jam with in high school, he was able to make pocket change from the occasional local gigs with them. But he'd always been taught by his dad that even if music was the most important thing in his life, he'd have to figure out something more solid to pay the bills. Bo continued to take gigs during college, but followed his father's advice. After all, his father had made a nice life for them by working in the insurance field, which held no appeal for Bo.

He answered an ad for a hospital registration clerk and was hired on the spot at New York County Memorial Hospital. It wasn't glamorous and it paid very little, but by the time he made supervisor two years later, it ultimately gave him the love of his life: Margret Sterling.

Early in their marriage, Bo was still taking gigs that sometimes required traveling. Margret opted to stay behind; it was cheaper.

He and his three college cronies – Pip Jones, Joey Fritz and Tim McKnight – were only a "quartet" in theory. It was impossible to get them all together anymore as they'd all spread out, so Bo looked for gigs on his own, whether it meant performing in front of an audience or studio work as a session player. The gigs had to be commutable. Fortunately, Brooklyn was close to a lot of desirable markets like upstate New York, Long Island, New Jersey and Pennsylvania.

Being a musician had a lot of rituals. He packed his wobbly luggage the night before with multiple sets of strings, three cakes of rosin (to keep the bow from sliding off the strings) and a small box of AA batteries for his music stand light. He also brought a few small towels to wipe his brow onstage, a water bottle with a tight top that could get knocked over without causing an electrical hazard, extra socks for changing between sets (nothing beat a pair of fresh, cool socks after a sweaty performance) and clothes. Traveling with an upright bass strewn across the collapsed back seat was its own specific migraine. Every time, he said a little prayer to keep it safe.

Rising at the sliver of dawn to shower and dress, Bo would lean over Margret (who, if it was a weekend, would still be in bed and under the covers) and quietly kiss her cheek. She'd smile and go back to sleep, pulling the sheet over her, oblivious of his admiration for her feminine form. On weekday gigs when he was about to leave, she was already up and heading to the shower. She'd give him a quick hug and wish him luck.

When the front door to their apartment closed, Margret could still detect a few molecules of his cologne that had stayed behind, lingering, watching over her. She'd breathe them in, hoping the scent- memory would last until he came back. A small moment of missing him would come and pass.

Per her request, Bo always called when he got to his hotel room no matter what time it was, though he'd rather let her sleep and then catch up in the morning.

There was no better thrill following a gnarly road trip to a strange city than arriving in your hotel room, closing the door on the rest of the world and flopping on a bed with new sheets. He always slept soundly that first night, no thoughts of worry over his upcoming performance. *It will be what it will be and then I'll go home.*

The work got his name "out there" and built his brand, no matter how futile it seemed, since the competition among musicians in New York City was notoriously beyond fierce. Usually the remuneration was very modest, barely covering his accommodations and meals. Coming out ahead was a rarity. Regardless of how he fared financially from the performances and the studio work, Bo always gave 110%, putting his game face on and cheerfully engaging audiences. Though not all musicians bothered to put in the extra effort, it was easy because he truly loved playing. He also knew that his enthusiasm made him a memorable commodity and it upped his appeal which led to more work.

Bo missed playing with his college buddies but those days were gone as everyone had spread out. He took every call for subbing with other musicians and appreciated the extra funds; these were their money-saving years, pre-kids, pre-house.

Although the work meant travelling all weekend with a short respite to actually play the bass, leaving him physically spent, it gave him a sort of creative and romantic energy that he took home. Margret looked forward to their end-of-weekend reunions as marriage boosters. There was nothing wrong with keeping the passion alive.

CHAPTER 6

"Did I ever tell you about Gramma Ida and the lullaby she sang to me when I was little?"

Bo was thinking about the photos in his Gramma's house when he was growing up. She was in most of them, and she had the widest, most beautiful smile he'd ever seen. He used to think her face was going to crack open.

"Nope, you never mentioned it. But I'm sure you're gonna tell me," said Margret with a chuckle. They had both just gotten home from work and neither was in the mood to cook, so it was going to be a mashup of leftovers.

"Okay, so here it is," he said. "Now look, I remember she used to sing me to sleep with this song, but it was very long ago, so if you think you're going to be slick and ask my dad to verify it, well, he probably won't remember. I don't even know if he ever heard her singing it to me. Those were our special times together, just Gramma and me."

"Well, okay," she observed, smelling a container of tortellini with marinara sauce and dumping it into a bowl. "So just sing me whatever you remember. Now you have me curious, and I kind of wish I knew this while she was still alive. I would have liked to hear her sing it."

"Seems like the funeral was only yesterday." Bo looked down and shook his head. "It's been three years already, and I miss her beyond what I can say."

His grandmother's passing had left a gaping hole in his life. Her special lullaby had touched his young heart in a way that was deep and permanent.

"So anyway, the song." He cleared his throat and started humming to find the right pitch. "Don't hold me to these words, but it's something like this:

The bird is full of hope;
She tends to her little ones.
When life gets hard
When she is torn up
She gets stronger.
She will fly to her duty
She will love with her whole heart
This bird full of hope."

Margret popped the bowl in the microwave and took out the cherry seltzer. It was hard work getting off the soda, certainly an addiction that came with no benefit. "That's beautiful!" she said. "She wrote this song, then? You never told me she was a poet."

Bo hunted for something else to eat and came up with an older leftover, further back in the fridge, which was an overstuffed baked potato. Everything had fallen out of it, but it could be pieced together and heated just fine. "Poet? I doubt it. She worked in a bubble gum factory in the 30s and then at the Dixie Bus Station in

Manhattan, if I'm not mistaken. But no, this is not her song."

"Do tell?"

"You know my great-great uncle was a slave who never saw emancipation, right?"

She nodded. "You mentioned it once."

"Gramma Ida attributed this song to him. His name was Lymus Jefferson Abbott and family legend says he played piano. She heard her mother sing it and I guess I inherited their love for music."

"You never told me about him. I can't imagine how you felt when you found out...I'm so sorry." She reached for his hand and brought it up to her lips to kiss it.

"I know, baby. It's just how it was."

They ate in silence. The song kept swirling around in Bo's head.

Singing it to his wife had awoken something that was kept buried for years, and this wasn't going to be the last time anyone heard it.

CHAPTER 7

On Johnkannaus, Master let us play our instruments, and sing, and oh what a time. They would keep an eye on us, still. We celebrated at dinnertime with our little flutes and guitars. We played from our hearts and laughed and for a time forgot about our hardships. But never did we forget we were still not free. I kept thinking that if I could be a 'monica player and get Master to sing maybe he would show mercy on our women and girls.

"What the heck is that, *Johnkannaus*? Have you ever heard of it?" asked Margret, who was helping Bo research slavery on the plantations. She'd managed to find a rare mention of music from the perspective of an enslaved person.

"Never in my life," said Bo. "It sounds kind of like their Christmas. I had no idea they would have been allowed any celebrations." Bo wondered if escapes were planned around that time of year, and if so, if they'd been successful. An ancient pain from somewhere inside made him want to reach back in time and pull his family members to safety, into emancipated times, even knowing they would face different issues today.

He wondered what Lymus was like, man to man. If he closed his eyes and listened closely enough, he could almost hear Lymus at the piano, picking out a melody, positioning his fingers into chords, singing along. More than 150 years later, would Lymus, looking at today's world, agree that society had moved into more enlightened days? Or just more deceptive days?

"It says here that the celebrants dressed in rags, sometimes in animal costumes. The meaning of the festival is lost but they think it originated in Africa," said Margret. Bo's eyes stung.

Margret long ago resigned herself to understanding that Bo, as a man who felt many things deeply and often at the same time, would slip into periods of sad reflection when it came to his family's past. Unfathomable daily struggles scarred his ancestors but also strengthened them, and this resiliency was passed down through generations. It found its way into his music, in his dedication to the craft.

Although Margret had nothing to compare from her own family tree, she knew to give Bo the time and space to be alone when his mind went to its dark corners. When he'd had enough and felt he was being pulled too far towards the center of the earth, he'd come up for air.

He was the type of man who gave and accepted love easily for which Margret was grateful. So many other men (they were boys, really) felt it was "soft" to be vulnerable. Bo made it clear he had no time for pretense.

"Come here," she motioned to Bo, placing her hand on the bed as she was getting dressed for work. She wore her pink scrubs for breast cancer awareness week.

Bo took a few steps toward her. She was sitting on the edge of the mattress.

Standing over her, he placed his hands lightly on her shoulders and kissed the top of her head. Her damp hair smelled like plums. He turned his gaze to the floor and saw her white nurse's shoes, the ones she told him felt like cotton clouds, peeking out from under the blanket. He smiled, happy to know that she was comfortable at her new job, but he missed having her nearby at work. She had walked into an insanely busy environment at St. Cecil's, but what hospital wasn't like that? Between his job at County as director of registration in the emergency room and her job in administration overseeing Radiology and a few smaller divisions, they were churnin' and burnin', building their nest, neither one looking to create any bumps in the road. Life, though, had other plans.

CHAPTER 8

Margret sat at a rooftop bar two months into her new job, celebrating a successful state audit with a few of her subordinates and the whole upper management team, all of whom believed it would be a mortal sin to pass on the free drinks and amazing view of the Empire State Building. Her department renewed its annual credentialing and was on the way to being named among the top 50 nationally for the first time in its history. She was sure this was in part due to her personal efforts. Since day one, she held her staff accountable for handing out patient satisfaction forms to every single patient and family member, logging in every one of them within 24 hours, and running stats on cleanliness, efficiency, how patients perceived the compassion of the MRI, X-ray and CT techs, and how quickly they received their results from the radiologists.

That was the easy part of the audit.

Margret also had to submit reports on the machinery in the department, which she oversaw. Everything had to be kept humming and in peak condition at all times. This unfortunately meant dealing with some very difficult vendors who were famous for sending different specialists every time. Most of them couldn't give two craps about precise calibrations, when they showed up at all. This headache intensified due to the risk of unreliable films, necessitating callbacks and re-takes that royally pissed off the patients. It was totally avoidable, strictly a matter of human error and laziness. The other challenges that factored into the hospital's ratings were staff turnover, training, procedural consistency and growing their patient numbers...as if she had any way to influence that in her department. Of course, her superiors didn't want to hear excuses.

She kept on top of the managers to make sure follow-ups were booked immediately and she was even expected to write some of the promo materials herself like the family-and-friend discount flyers which should have been Marketing's job. Word had somehow gotten out that she could write, so they looked to her first before bothering anyone else.

St. Cecil's had gotten savvy and realized patients liked freebies. Drawing in new patients seemed to be worth the tiny budget devoted to bulk-ordering hospital-logoed bookbags, water bottles, baseball caps and a pink rose for all mammogram patients. *So that's what Marketing does here,* she thought.

The biggest pressure was the day-to-day scrutiny over improving the department's "weeklies," the Monday-to-Friday stats that showed up red (bad) or green (good) on the VP's whiteboard. The redder the board looked, the more Margret's stomach clenched anticipating the late Friday afternoon phone calls with the VP of Finance.

It was a balmy evening with a few dashes of orange and purple in the sky, the sun setting behind skyscrapers. She looked around at her crew. They were good people, easy to be with, hard workers. That was a godsend. But there's always one wild card in the bunch, and that was Dennis, a recently hired ultrasound tech who had to be broken in big-time. She gave him the benefit of the doubt and offered a warm welcome. "Glad you could make it tonight. Would you look at that sky!"

Dennis was a recent college grad and really just wanted his 9 to 5, and sometimes not even that. It was beastly to hear him complain about rotating to second shift. The scheduling was done as fairly as possible, and everybody had to rotate to evenings once a month. But Dennis didn't go down without a fight. He wore a sort of arrogance often seen in the young and privileged (his entire degree was paid for by his dad, a divorce attorney who practiced in Short Hills, New Jersey), and on his first day, he explained to Margret that he should be exempt from the rotation because of unspecified "obligations at home." Not only did he feel he should be allowed to skip among the daisies; he also believed it was his right to flirt whenever the mood struck him. Nobody gave him the time of day, and his presence was already becoming detrimental to morale. Margret knew she had to do something about it. She was no fan of stupidity in the workplace, so at the next hint of swagger she called him in to read him the riot act. "This is a no-drama workplace," she stated as his smirk began to droop. "We're a family here. A good attitude, and that includes the appropriate respect shown to your co-workers and supervisor, goes a long way here." She paused for effect. His blink rate had increased. *Ah, I've gotten through.* "Your success here is not guaranteed, but when you get off to a strong start, somehow the best advancement opportunities become available. You get me?" Dennis's neck reddened and he nodded. "We encourage and empower our staff to be their best selves and make a great career here."

It seemed like he got the drift and he started behaving more professionally. Margret even noticed his co-workers warming up to him, most evident in their willingness to swap holidays and days off.

Life as a supervisor had constant personnel blips, so Margret enlisted the help of six pumps of espresso in an oversized coffee every morning. She came bounding into work with purpose and a caffeine-fueled smile. It wasn't until early afternoon that she lagged a bit and needed some refreshment in the form of a second (but smaller) cup of coffee and a walk around the campus to the mailroom to get her department's mail. It reset her energy level for the remainder of the afternoon. It also gave her time to think about Bo.

Lately, she was concerned about his growing interest in Lymus Abbott's life, and while this wasn't a problem in itself, it seemed to dampen his spirits overall. She'd just have to keep an eye on it.

CHAPTER 9

St. Cecil's had more layers than an epicure's lasagna: Margret headed up the Women's Center, and a newbie named Bobby Slovitz was hired to be her boss over the entire radiology division, a position typically earned through many years in the trenches. The secret sauce here was his uncle, who sat fat and happy on the board of directors.

It wasn't only that his people skills were lacking and that he had no practical experience heading up a radiology department. The biggest problem that Margret observed right off the bat was his "disco mentality" – leaving his shirt unbuttoned, revealing a scruff of unsightly chest hair; tight polyester dress pants (*where did he find his threads, from a time machine?* she thought) and poor hygiene. It started with too much cologne (the hospital was officially a fragrance-free environment, but apparently those at the top were exempt despite the coughing fits of the peons). Then there were the sweaty semi-circles under his armpits and another unappealing swatch of sweat on his back. He flossed at meetings and combed his hair often, like a tic. Margret was fully disgusted.

"Wait it out," Bo told her. "He probably won't last long, even with that uncle of his."

"Or he'll be promoted," she said.

"One can only hope."

Bo was having his own personnel issues at work that would prove to be much more serious than bad attitudes and perspiration.

CHAPTER 10

Aimee was one of the quiet ones on Bo's staff at New York County Memorial.

She started her career there two years earlier, in housekeeping. It was a foot in the door, she told herself. A newly minted college graduate who still lived at home, she eked out one hundred dollars to contribute towards her mother's rent.

Aimee wanted more: more financial stability, her own apartment and a more exciting social life. Her mom was great company, but it was impossible to bring guys home. And since Aimee was smart, charming and had a classic, dark-eyed gorgeousness, there were lots of guys who wanted to go home with her.

Getting her own place couldn't come quickly enough.

When nearly eight months later an opening was posted in dietary services at the next salary grade, she applied immediately.

Her supervisor had called her "dedicated and punctual." HR moved fast. Within a week of applying, Aimee found herself in a new uniform delivering meals to patients throughout the hospital. Her favorite sections were the neonatal unit, feeding the exhausted new moms, and the pediatric oncology wing. She delivered the trays with a smile, trying to infuse a little bit of joy in every room. Silently, every day, she thanked God she was not the one on the receiving end.

It was fulfilling, a role she could settle into. Her co-workers were friendly, her boss was never around, and she got plenty of exercise by taking the stairs to keep her trim figure.

About a year later, with Aimee about to finish college and hoping to move out soon, her mom – who had, for nearly a decade, suffered through a dismal time as a widow – started dating a new man. It looked serious and her mother talked about getting remarried. Aimee realized she'd have to up her game as soon as possible to be able to get her own apartment.

She was in luck. The hospital had just posted openings for registration representatives in the ER, which the media called the second busiest in Manhattan. The salary would be an appreciable bump up. She applied and, thanks to her stellar performance evaluations, was offered the job. Another plus: she'd heard that a really cute guy ran the department.

CHAPTER 11

Matt Singelli had never seen a more beautiful student.

Every year's crop of co-eds was sensational, and he looked forward to starting a new semester to pick out the beautiful women in his classes. This time seemed different. There was something about Aimee Patel that drew the professor in like a moth to a flame.

Aimee had signed up for Singelli's history class in her final semester to fulfill her social sciences requirement. It seemed like the least onerous class. Everybody knew he was an easy grader and not too shabby to look at. Within a few months, she would emerge with her Bachelor of Science in bio and could start to apply for jobs at County Memorial. Prof. Singelli's class was the most direct route to a respectable GPA.

What she didn't count on was coffee with the professor at his invitation just two weeks into class. Aimee fell into the ocean of blue in his eyes. He had perfectly flecked salt-and-pepper hair and a soul patch which her friends thought was ridiculous (Aimee found it sexy). He must be at least fifty, she guessed. Maybe the little square of facial hair on his chin made him feel young.

Singelli was also incredibly fit; an ex-Marine who had served during the Gulf War. He started teaching in an unexpected way. A history buff for as long as he could remember, he started his career with a series of uninspiring retail jobs. Once he enlisted, he became the resident history whiz. He poured out his knowledge of Asia and the Middle East to anyone who'd listen, lending a cultural perspective that gave his fellow soldiers context; they weren't just plopped into a part of the world they had no understanding of. He could expound on language (he spoke six), art, music and military history. After serving his four years, he decided to go back to civilian life, just not back to retail. With a deep interest in history, teaching seemed as good a choice as any. He pursued a master's and went on to get a PhD.

The good professor had managed to stay single all these years and he kind of enjoyed an uncomplicated personal life. One night when he was marking papers, he came across hers and felt something that he hadn't felt in a long time. Arousal. Suddenly he couldn't stop thinking about Aimee – her long, glossy hair and sexy smile. He agonized over asking her out and how it would be a risky move, but then reasoned to himself that she wouldn't be an undergrad for long. The next day, after a few furtive glances back and forth during class, fueling the fire, he waited for his chance. She stayed behind to pack her book bag, which he took as the classic sign of interest. She looked up and smiled at him, which he thought was another sign, so he asked her to breakfast for the following day. To his surprise, she stared right into his baby blues and without hesitation responded "I'd love to, Matt." Hearing his name come from those lovely plump lips caused tingles to fizzle up his neck. This was certainly promising. She might even be the one; after all, he wasn't getting any younger.

It was just one cup of coffee on the pretense of discussing recent archeological discoveries in Southeast Asia. Aimee didn't much care for the subject matter – he already knew she was taking his class to get her last remaining credits – but she held his gaze with an impressive directness for a twenty-year-old. She agreed with her classmates: he was easy on the eyes. Then all of a sudden, he was growing on her.

Once they started dating, Aimee got a vibe that Matt was going to propose fairly soon. He talked a lot about his married friends and how he wanted to find the right woman, and while he didn't seem desperate, he was 54 and time was ticking.

Aimee told her friends she loved him, just without all the sentiment and fanfare. Maybe this is love *for me*, she thought. She cared about him. He'd be a good provider and he absolutely adored her. She didn't share his level of emotional passion but she felt certain it would eventually blossom into true love.

If he proposed, she decided she'd say yes. Being married would give her life more structure, having somebody by her side as she took the first steps of her career. A good-looking, and tenured professor, somebody she'd be comfortable coming home to. No more having to avoid the hard-drinking party animals who acted more like boys than grown men.

CHAPTER 12

Bo welcomed Aimee to the registration team and all seemed fine at first. Through bits and pieces of conversation, she learned he was more than just a casual musician. He had majored in performance in college and minored in composition. He played in a jazz band in his 20s and even got some local press. This was all before he decided to get into healthcare. "If only I'd have stuck with it, maybe I'd be touring with Wynton and playing at Birdland," he told her. He wasn't sure why he spoke so freely to her about music. Maybe it had something to do with the engagement ring on her finger that allowed him to let his guard down and be friendly without looking lecherous.

When he talked about jazz, Aimee noticed his face lit up. She found herself bringing up the topic whenever they ran into each other. "I still play when I can," he told her. "It keeps me grounded, and I know this is a cliché, but it makes me feel like all things are possible."

He was referring to music, but Aimee took it another way, as if (she thought) he was dropping a hint. *I'll show you what is possible, Mr. Adorable.*

CHAPTER 13

"Guess who landed a gig?"

Margret was about to go into a department meeting. "Thank God somebody has good news," she said quietly into her phone. "I have this meeting with Slovitz in two minutes. Tell me quick."

"Remember the little kid from Queens I used to give lessons to, Jackie Carter?"

"Mmm hmm?"

"Well, I must've made a good impression back then. Turns out he's a bigwig at the Met, and his folks are having a vow renewal ceremony at the ballroom. Which bass player do you think they want?"

Margret nodded to the head of Cardiology passing her doorway who motioned for her to hurry up. "Be right there," she whispered.

"The Metropolitan Opera?" Margret was stunned. This would be a great place for Bo to meet some musical movers and shakers and possibly land some side jobs. He missed performing. It had been a long dry spell.

Bo explained it was the Metropolitan Museum of Art. *Well, still very cool,* thought Margret. The curators, exhibit designers and donors...it sounded like a mega opportunity.

"I didn't realize you were still in the market, but it sounds amazing." She grabbed a notebook and stood up. Now she really had to get going.

"I'll take this kind of gig every time," he said. "It's $400 for the night for me, and they're having three other musicians." Margret tapped on the desk.

"I don't know these guys from Adam," Bo continued. "Anyway, I have two weeks or so to practice and I've got every jazz fake book imaginable, so I am all set."

"And if that tux from the Year One is still around somewhere in the closet from hell, you won't have to rent one. But I need to go."

"I'll let you run," he said. "See you later. Love ya."

Bo looked up and saw Aimee coming into the office.

"Hi." She smiled at him.

"Hey. How's the floor?" *All business, no personal stuff. No more talk about the bass.*

"We knocked out all the registrations in the overdose section," she said, not taking her eyes off him. "Must've been quite an evening last night." The way she looked at him made him slightly uncomfortable. Still, he wasn't entirely displeased. This was confusing.

Aimee sat down and sucked on her Diet Pepsi. "So, you said you like jazz and you used to play bass. Do you play anything now?"

Yeah. I play a married man on TV.

"Still bass," he said, resigned to this line of conversation. "I cut my teeth on violin, though." Why did he tell her that, and open the door to more conversation? His eyes went to his computer screen, hoping to find new patients who needed to be registered. All was quiet.

"Well, I do community theater here and there. Not really a fan of jazz, but I can learn." Aimee had a smile she let fade, almost as if she wanted him to catch it and wonder what she was thinking.

Silence was not his friend. Babbling took its place.

"I'm into this old timer named Stef Dalton. I guess you could say he's my idol. He's been with some pretty exciting bands and has a signature sound that just knocks my socks off."

While the pretty young registration rep couldn't care less, she was enjoying this private conversation. *So cute! And that body. Man is into fitness! I'll just linger with my Pepsi and see how things roll.*

The screen lit up. Thanks be to God. "Oh, look at this," he said, getting up from his chair. "Three patients with lice. Grab your latexes and gown up. Let me know if you need help."

CHAPTER 14

Bo wasn't used to playing at a formal event and was even less accustomed to wearing a bow tie. The last time he was at the Metropolitan Museum of Art was three years back, with Margret's sister Claire and her kids. Bo had steered them to the musical instrument rooms and drooled like a hungry lion over the harpsichords and the lutes. He never thought the sprawling institution could be a source of income for him.

The press was there, the Met's well-heeled donors were there, and droves of guests in stifling attire were there, all trying to navigate the crowded ballroom. *These people sure have a lot of friends,* he thought. *Or else they want to impress a lot of people.*

He ran a finger under his collar, which was buttoned all the way up. It would probably bother him for the entire evening, but this was too interesting a crowd to worry about a little temporary discomfort. If nothing else, he could people-watch while making some bucks to play a few songs. Not a bad way to spend a few hours.

Despite the best efforts of the building manager, the air conditioner wasn't cutting it. Too many people per square foot caused a collective body warmth that couldn't be dissipated.

Later on, he'd be relieved to yank off the bow tie and slog out of the silk-lined jacket. For now, it was showtime. He started tuning up his bass.

It was his first time meeting the other instrumentalists in person, although they'd spoken by Zoom once to review the playlist. One thing that amused Bo was the leader's warning to keep solos to no more than eight bars, and improvising in other keys was verboten. "Stay on the root, guys!" he said. That was just plain stupid. But just thinking of the little wad of cash he'd come out with and the chance to get his hands on some of the fat pink shrimp over ice was going to make it all worth it.

There was something else. Deep into the second song, a watered-down version of Frank Sinatra's "Summer Wind," he rediscovered his element. The last time he played in an ensemble was about a dozen years ago at Margret's cousin's kid's bar mitzvah. The kid dug jazz, and Bo's quartet was hardly overbooked. The Rosenfelds couldn't be happier. They'd be that hip Jewish family who turned away from the current tide of hip-hop and rap at these parties, daring to bring some cookin' jazz to the 13-year-old set. There were no dirty lyrics to deal with. Maybe the kids would get some culture.

The guests were starting to loosen their ties; unfortunately, Bo was not allowed to follow their lead. Little by little they drifted over to the dance floor to enjoy the music, which, in Bo's mind, played it totally safe with a blend of Sinatra, Cole Porter, Gershwin and, to spice things up (he supposed), a little Cab Calloway with some guy he hadn't seen before jumping in to do the throaty vocals.

He didn't know how much more time they'd play for but it was already enough to reignite his passion for performing. It would be great to do more events if he got the chance; even get his old friends together somehow and this time totally let loose with some authentic improv.

Bo was really getting in the mood when the emcee (it was incredible that a renewing of vows ceremony needed a narrator) looked at the piano player and made a slicing gesture to his throat. "No, no, no!" thought Bo. It was right before the trombone sassed out after Calloway's famous "Hi-di-hi" riff. It felt like a cardiac surgeon putting down her scalpel just as she was about to make a chest incision.

"Hello you beautiful people!" began the music-killer. "Thank you all for showing up tonight. We're here to celebrate a very exciting 40 years of wedded bliss for Ben and Anne Carter. Let's hear it for the lovey-dovey couple!"

The musicians had abandoned their instruments and quietly made their way to the delightful platter after platter of free food: glistening shrimp, chicken satay skewers, truffle risotto pies, penne pasta with different sauces...it was probably the most food any of them had seen at a gig. The pianist, a silver-ponytailed guy from across the river in Hoboken, talked with his mouth full. "Grab what you can. We go back on in 15."

Bo stepped out of the ballroom and sat on a brown velvet loveseat balancing two small plates mounded with mouth-watering, perfect bites. A few feet away, four gruff men were laughing and cutting each other off in conversation. He tried not to eavesdrop but it was too tempting.

"Fetterman's new play, did you hear about it?" asked one.

"What, that thing from the 1920s? Who advised him on that!" said another, to which a third man responded, "It was a flop then, why should it be any different now? I mean, unless he has a better director than his other plays, and also, you know, it's not very PC."

"I gotta tell you." The first man again. "I think old Bernie found himself some new composer from the Czech Republic or someplace like that. We'll just have to see. You know how critics are, though. Bru-Tal."

"Yeah," agreed another. "Imagine, the opera that 'dared to' go up against *Porgy and Bess*. I hope for his sake there's an audience for it today."

Bo's ears perked up. *Porgy and Bess* was one of his favorite operas and now it made him think of the era immediately following Lymus's passing. It was a whitewashed version of history, granted, but the music, not the scripting, interested him.

"Son of a bitch," said the Czech Republic guy. "Look who's rolling over now."

They all turned to see an old bloke in a wheelchair being pushed by a woman with a helmet of hay-colored hair and unnaturally furry eyelashes.

"Speak of the devil! Bernie Fetterman! How the fuck are you?"

The glad-handing had begun. The posse of yentas converged on the aging producer, each seeking validation and approval. At least a handshake.

Fetterman was looking right at Bo. "And who are you?"

"I'm the bassist. And you are...?"

The posse laughed nervously.

"I just produced the greatest revival ever, Mister Bow Ttie. *The Scandals of Violet*. Ever hear of it?"

Bo couldn't understand why he had this man's attention, especially when he was surrounded by so many eager admirers. Plus, he had to get back onstage for the next set (better stated as *music to eat dinner by*).

"Young man. I heard you playing up there, and you bring to mind a young, who was it? A young Charlie Mingus."

"That is a huge compliment. I'm humbled. Thank you." Bo moved in to shake hands. "I do birthdays and bar mitzvahs too." He gave it a shot.

Fetterman chuckled. "Well, listen. You and those musicians out there. I want you to come to my opening. Here—" He put his hand behind him and swatted at the woman who was pushing the wheelchair. "Lottie, give this young man four tickets for his musician friends."

"How long've you been together?" The man smelled rich, like a fresh shower in just-plucked peonies, and he was dressed to the nines. His teeth (dentures? implants?) were brilliantly whitened. He even wore spats.

"I'm just a plug-in for tonight, man, and we kind of just met. But we're cookin', aren't we?"

"Damn right you are. So here. I think you'll enjoy yourself. Now let me get back to these sycophants."

That was a stunner. According to the tickets, the premier of Fetterman's show was in two weeks. One ticket though. Margret wouldn't mind. They could go into the city early, catch some dinner, and she could go home after.

This Fetterman character seemed to like him. Maybe he'd need a stand-in if he used a live orchestra. You never knew what an encounter like this could lead to.

The last thing on Bo's mind, that he didn't yet know, was that the universe had brought him directly to two people – the big, fancy producer and his wife – who played a key role in his great-great uncle's legacy.

CHAPTER 15

"You're sure you don't mind me going to see this play without you?" Bo asked Margret, who was gingerly folding a blouse next to her open suitcase on the bed. The next three days would be devoted to her first annual out-of-town convention and trade show for hospital technologists. This year it was in Minneapolis. It had come up with basically no notice (that was how things worked at St. Cecil's) and thanks to Murphy's Law, coincided with opening night of *Scandals of Violet*. He was at least hoping they could go into the city together, but then this.

"I don't mind at all," she said. "A free ticket is nothing to sneeze at. Maybe you'll see some celebs."

The blouse packed better by rolling it up inside a small towel. She had to get a few pairs of pantyhose and clear nail polish for runs, her dress shoes (she wouldn't fly all dressed up) and an extra skirt. She was determined to get everything into a carry-on.

"The play might not be very PC, you know that, right?" she asked. Funny, the old guys had even said this. "If you say it was written around *Porgy and Bess*, there might be some dicey subject matter," she added.

"I know. Actually, I'm pretty interested in how Fetterman is going to portray people of color. But I'm also really looking forward to the music."

She walked over to the closet to take another blouse off a hanger, leaning into Bo as she passed him. They locked lips. Her man always smelled fresh and spicy, all at the same time.

"I'm hoping to avoid Slovitz as much as possible," she said. "Thank God some people will be there from St. Cecil's."

"Oh yeah? Who?"

"I don't know yet. I saw the list of attendees, but it didn't name who, just that Cecil's is there with the number seven; that leaves five other possible allies. Anybody would be better than Slovitz." She stuck her tongue out.

"Well, besides the play, I've got nothing going on this week, so I'll do all the laundry and meal-prep stuff. Maybe I'll pull out old Chauncey and start noodling around again. The Met reminded me how much I love playing." Chauncey was the name he'd given to his bass.

"Send me a clip on your phone when you get seated tomorrow night, just don't get caught or they'll throw you out. I'm sure I could use the entertainment. Although," she added, "my idol August Jamison will be there giving a presentation. I signed up for the breakout session he's leading." Margret subscribed to his YouTube channel. He was the definitive source on business-to-consumer diagnostics in radiology.

"Hmm. Should I be jelly of Jamison? You gonna behave?"

She folded four pairs of underwear into little triangles and threw one pair in his face. "Yeah, for sure. *Trends in Radiology* – so hot, I might just skip the undies and go commando."

CHAPTER 16

Margret usually took off the anniversary of her mother's death, but she had to be at the radiology convention. In three more days, it would be Saturday. They take the LIRR deep into Long Island and grab a cab the rest of the way to the cemetery. It was exactly what Margret wouldn't feel like doing after being away from home and having to endure her boss.

The days when her mom was at her worst were soul-wrenching for everybody, and Margret, at the tender age of eleven, had taken her mother's early death the hardest.

Patricia Ann Sterling had been hospitalized in a psychiatric facility for three years by the time she passed away. A raging alcoholic, she caused permanent and substantial damage to her family by disappearing for weeks at a time to wander the east Bronx. Somehow her husband Paul, desperate and determined, was able to take control of the situation and finally had her admitted.

The only family members she would allow to visit besides her husband was Margret, who was named after Patricia's own mother. The other three children were excluded; nobody ever figured out why. Scars formed on their little hearts, eventually producing adult-sized problems.

Paul Sterling, straining to be optimistic, drove all four children to the hospital every Saturday. It was a forlorn-looking institution which had no energy for pretense. A residence for alcoholics and the mentally unstable – whose families had tried everything else – to go and die. Paul took Margret by the hand and led her through the front doors where she'd start to gag, the foul-smelling air inside almost knocking down her little frame. Margret's two brothers and her sister Claire stayed behind in the car with their Uncle Ross, who was tasked with keeping them occupied and deflecting the stifling atmosphere of melancholy. This visit, those doors, that smell. Margret was going down a deep, dark rabbit hole when her phone buzzed.

"Hey, sweets. How's it going? Got time for a chat?" It was Bo.

Margret could tell he was beaming. The dark vapors dissipated.

"Perfect timing. I'm thinking about my mom and our long trip to the Island on Saturday. I'm dreading all of it. So what's up?" Margret had just returned to her room. There was a break between workshops and she was dying to get out of her heels and flop on her bed. She had a half hour until the next presentation and for now, the only thing in the world she wanted was to be shoeless.

Bo had already texted her first thing in the morning to tell her to have a great day and to say *sorry about your Mom, I love you.*

"I got some practice time in with Chauncey last night. I'm really rusty. But it's okay."

"Nice. Are you getting dressed up for the play tonight?"

"Nah. Nobody does that anymore. But I'm so excited. I almost looked it up on YouTube to watch the trailer but I don't want to spoil it. I want to hear it fresh when it's live."

Margret was lying on her hotel bed cushioned by six pillows and she didn't even have to share any. It was luscious. She cradled the phone between her ear and her shoulder and let Bo lullaby her.

"I brought my jeans and another shirt and I'm going straight from work," he added. "This day is dragging! But enough about me. Did you work that auditorium to the hilt yet? Networking your little tushy off?"

Margret chuckled. "Nope. Actually, it's been pretty boring so far. But this afternoon we'll have August Jamison speaking about emerging technology and a new imaging that can show cancers much earlier. Pretty amazing stuff."

Bo looked over to the ER nurse's station and saw a lot of activity. His screen suddenly glowed red. That meant ambulance patients were coming in hand over fist. "Trauma alert, ETA four minutes" crackled the loudspeaker.

"Mags, I gotta run. Miss you, love you."

"Okie dokes. Love ya back." Margret turned her head and saw the clock had somehow advanced fifteen minutes. Time to spruce herself up and see what Mr. Jamison had to say.

Bo watched the screen as the registration reps wasted no time clicking on each room.

Let this day end already, and please, no more Aimee for the day. I just can't.

CHAPTER 17

Bo threaded his way to the fifth row, center orchestra. Fetterman must've been out of his mind to give out a ticket like that for free. Actually, four tickets.

He saw two of the musicians from the night at the Met. "Hey man, how are you?"

"Bo, right?" It was the maniacal pianist from Hoboken. "I'm Dex."

"Nice to see you. I've got a distant relative named Dex. Pretty big in the jazz world in the Carolinas, I've heard."

The pianist was a skinny dude who kept his hands folded in his lap, and to the other side of Bo was a little girl of about seven who cuddled over to her mom, so both armrests were his for the taking. To Hoboken's right was the sax player from the gig at The Met who barely smiled. The drummer was nowhere to be seen. Maybe he had scalped his ticket. The trombonist didn't get a ticket, but he was a walk-on for the Calloway piece so Fetterman forgot to throw him one.

The sights, smell and feel of the theater were an instant transport to his youth, when he and Pip Jones would cut school at Madison High School in Brooklyn, hop on the Number 1 or 2 train, and head over to the theater district just to catch a glimpse of the Broadway musicians as they entered through the back door. As they lugged their instruments forward, they failed to notice the two malingerers. Bo and Pip saved just enough money from their part-time burger-flipping jobs to see exactly one play, "Evita," on the week it was set to close. The musical score by Andrew Lloyd Weber was so awe-inspiring that Bo cried after the last curtain call. Pip made fun of him for it, but his own eyes were glistening.

The lights flickered. There would be no more conversation or reminiscing.

Bo let the day melt off him. As the room darkened, the live orchestra – such a rare treat – led with the strings into a light, classical tune as the conductor and his musicians continued their smooth mechanical descent into the pit. The music became more robust. Bo's skin prickled. This was the overture.

The score of *Scandals* had already set a mood of nostalgia and romance. Bo silently sipped his glass of dry red wine as he scanned the set which was nothing short of miraculous: a sweeping vista of a Civil War-era plantation studded with magnolias and weeping willows, an immense Victorian mansion and off to the side, the slaves' quarters.

He knew he was in for a ride, and reminded himself to keep an open mind. This was the playwright's imaginings of a particular time set to music by a composer of that time, with lyrics that reflected the prevalent opinions and sensibilities of the era.

The first act consisted of eight scenes, the first seven of which could only be described as "breathtaking." The actors, many of them black (some of whom likely had a similar lineage to Bo), could have rationalized their participation in this play as professionals enacting a period piece. What seemed strikingly offensive and unenlightened was placed momentarily aside in service to the story.

The Playbill had mapped out one more scene before intermission. It began silently: an ultramarine sky shimmered gradually to a robin's egg blue, with cotton puffs that grew in number to give the impression of a sunrise. As the orchestra launched into full-on lyricism, a trumpet solo pierced the air. Bo felt an electric jolt followed by an unstoppable stream of words in his head which he found himself mumbling: *"The bird is full of hope. She tends to her young..."*

He was suddenly glued in place as the room began to swirl around him. To his left, and the little girl had nodded off on her mother's arm. To his right, Dex and the sax player were bopping gently and tapping their feet.

Bo remained unable to move, even a flicker. Dex leaned over and whispered, "Hey man, you know this piece?" "Yeah," said Bo, managing only one syllable. *I know it all too well.*

A mix of acid and fury rose up through his esophagus, but Bo was determined to ride it out. The rest of the play was as amazing as the first – technically tight, musically imaginative (if derivative, he mused) and thematically, he hated to admit, well-written. The playwright had brought an old tale into the present day in a meta sort of way, examining itself with sensitivity. Multiple disclaimers about the controversial content appeared in the Playbill and in one of the actor's fleeting lines. It was not lost on any of the adults in the audience.

At the inevitable standing ovation, Bo stood too, but only to exit, which he did without a word to his acquaintances. He stepped out into a theater district throbbing in neon. Instead of hailing a cab he decided to walk, pointing himself to the next subway stop.

A street musician was plying his trade with a violin, immersed in a Brandenburg Concerto. He swayed dramatically as he bowed his strings.

Bo extracted a ten-dollar bill from his pocket, stooped down to place it in the velvet-lined case and nodded to the musician, who nodded back.

For the next twelve city blocks Bo cried soundlessly. He tumbled down the subway stairs, caught the train and got off in Brooklyn. Still numb, he took himself straight to bed. No thoughts of calling Margret, no thoughts of anything but music.

CHAPTER 18

The phone played a cloying guitar tune, its cheerfulness meriting being hurled against a wall. Bo resisted.

He leaned over to the nightstand and dismissed the alarm. There was a text from Margret. "Good morning, happy Thursday. Hope you liked the play. Let me know you're alive? LOVE U 4E."

His brain fog lifted abruptly as he recalled the previous evening. He was still trying to make sense of it as he dialed Margret; at the same time, he made his way over to the coffee pot to prepare his needed libation. Always good for two cups before leaving the house, he'd put the rest in a thermos and draw off it during the day. *I need it strong today, for damn sure.*

At the tone, Bo spoke his message. He wasn't sure how to phrase it without bumming her out so early in the day, especially with her being away at the convention with her colleagues. "Hey babe, sorry I didn't text last night." The emotions were already percolating. "I'm fine, getting ready for another ER circus. The play was...really interesting. I'll fill you in later. Love ya and have a great one."

They knew each other too well, where an inflection, a hesitation, a word choice or word avoidance spoke volumes. Margret immediately understood something was wrong. It wasn't until the 10:30 a.m. break between sessions that she was able to call him back.

"Hey. You sound terrible. What's up?"

"Let me get into the office, hang on." Then: "You will not believe this. I just don't know where to start."

"Start anywhere. Did you get hurt?"

"Nothing like that. So the play, it was all-around pretty good. But right before intermission..." His voice broke. "They fucking stole Lymus's song."

The utterance hung in the air for several beats. Margret couldn't make sense of what he'd just said.

"What do you mean?"

Bo was about to punch a wall but realized he was at work. He took the furthest desk from the door and turned to the wall he wanted to put his fist through and spilled the details. "It was undeniably *that song*. Not just the melody, either - even the words. I just can't believe what I heard. That goddamned Fetterman. A disgusting thief. Two times over!"

Margret was nearly speechless. "What do you mean by two times?"

"Well, I'm going to do some research today and find out whatever I can about this play when it first debuted. Somehow, he copped Lymus's music and called it his own. Back then in 1934, and now in this revival."

Margret was at a long table in the back of the auditorium crammed with breakfast items for the conference attendees. She took two mini cinnamon buns and a scoop of scrambled eggs with what looked like factory-extruded squares of green pepper. She really wanted a cup of coffee but didn't have an extra hand for it. "What are you going to do? Really, what can you do?" she asked, balancing phone, plate and handbag.

Two registration reps entered the office and saw Bo on the phone. It looked like a personal call. They backed out.

"I don't know yet. But I want to speak to Zack about it. And I don't know if I can 'do' anything. It's just unbelievable. I'm seriously struggling to put on my game face here."

"Zack, your lawyer friend from college? I haven't heard you mention him in a while."

"Yeah. We keep up. He'll know how to put this in perspective."

"Oh God. I feel terrible. Do you want me to leave early? I can just cut out right now." Margret looked around the room. Bobby Slovitz caught her eye and waved. "Crap. Guess who's coming over."

"The Slob? Ooh baby, he likes you..." Bo lightened up momentarily.

"Gross. Really, hon, I can leave right now. Say the word."

He thought about it for a second. "No. I'm fine. Stay, enjoy your eggs and the sessions, and tell Slovvy you got your period and have to go lie down. That'll shut him up."

"Great advice. Here I go." She giggled.

"Don't worry about me. I'll see you tomorrow afternoon. Your thing ends at noon? So, between the flight home and the cab you'll be home like..."

"Dinnertime, and Bo, I love you so much. But you already knew that."

Bo took another deep breath and went out into the hallway. The registration reps were standing at their COWs (short for Computers On Wheels, but some manager high up on the food chain decided this wasn't politically correct and told people to say the whole name; still, everybody used the acronym). They were discussing their favorite Netflix series when the office door swung open. "C'mon in, I'm all done." Bo forced a smile. "Thanks for giving me some space."

Aimee had joined the group. Her timing left a lot to be desired. Apparently, there were no new patients on the screen and her radar told her Bo was in the office. "You okay?" she asked, passing him by to get to their mini-fridge.

She's a nosy little thing, he thought. *She's probably wondering if I was fighting on the phone with Mags.*

"As they say, 'I'm OK, You're OK,'" he intoned.

"I guess," she said vapidly. Too young; she missed the reference. It was a book he could use right about now.

CHAPTER 19

Zachary Adams was Bo's high school buddy. When Bo was laying down tracks in his bedroom with his wonky rented bass, a second-hand mic and a cassette recorder, Zack could be found with his nose in a book. Always studying, that kid. When you'd ask what he was reading, the answer was always different. Zack had a curiosity about the world that was never satisfied. He had no use for fiction; it was law, philosophy, psychology, religion, history, physics and medicine that grabbed him. Jurisprudence had somehow risen to the top and 2002 found him graduating third in his class at Brooklyn Law. No surprise that he flew through his bar exam and passed on the first try.

Bo and Zack stayed friends and enjoyed the pleasantries of reminiscing whenever they caught up. "Just wait until you're playing in a jazz club," Zack had told him when they were both single. "You'll be a chick magnet extraordinaire. You'll be fighting them off when all the jocks from Roosevelt High are getting osteoarthritis and knee replacements."

Although music didn't turn out to be his career path, Bo was gratified that he never strayed too far from it, or from his friend.

Now Zack worked at a high-end intellectual property firm in Los Angeles. He had migrated west, and along the way picked up a stunning wife (who was a dentist) and brand-new, twin baby girls. His career was on fire. He was, as one might say, "the shit."

Bo knew that if anybody had an inkling what to do about a possible stolen song, it would be Zack. At least he could put Bo on the right path.

"Zack the Whack!" Bo said when his friend came on the line.

"How the frig are ya?" Zack still sounded like he was 15.

Bo summarized the past two years, although Zack knew most of it anyway since they followed each other on social media: the vacations, the anniversaries, the new jobs, the new homes and their newfound culinary pursuits.

Bo unleashed the whole unbelievable saga of meeting Bernard Fetterman at the Carters' vow renewal gala at the Met, getting a ticket to his play and hearing a song that he swore was written by his great-great uncle. "I swear, this song is 100% Lymus Abbott."

Zack was silent. Bo could hear him drumming on his desk.

"Okay, Bo, let's just say this is the real deal. So, it's what we call the WOW law."

"Explain?"

Zack drew a breath. "Who Owns What. It deals with items or ideas that are over 150 years old, going all the way back into ancient times. It's an extremely complex specialty."

"Have you represented the descendants of slaves, regarding intellectual property?"

"Only once," said Zack. "The case was over a series of paintings about everyday slave life. The artist, supposedly, was an enslaved girl they called 'Jessina'."

"Bottom line, how did it turn out?" Bo asked.

Zack didn't think Bo was going to like the answer. He told Bo that although the current family members owned other items signed by Jessina which seemed to prove her signature (one could never be absolutely sure), there were no birth records, death certificates or other documents proving the lineage down to the family who brought the suit. They could have come to the paintings through friends of the family or even at a yard sale, and the signature was unfortunately something always left to interpretation.

"It died on the vine," said Zack. "But don't lose heart, my friend. There is this little-known piece of legislation called the Negro Enslavement Artifacts Act from, would you believe, 1952. Most people never heard of it."

A ray of hope.

"Let me do some research and I'll get back to you," Zack said. "Give my best to Mags. She around?"

"No, she's finishing up this radiology convention in Minneapolis. She'll be home tomorrow. I'll tell her you said hi. All my love to Desiree and the girls."

CHAPTER 20

Margret was relieved to be back home and gave her husband an extra-long hug. He needed one as well. Aimee had rushed through her registrations to haunt the office, hoping he'd be around. Bo had made himself scarce, camping out by the ambulance bay for most of the day.

"I'm exhausted," Margret said, heading into the bedroom. "I'm not even sure I want to drag myself all the way to the cemetery tomorrow. In fact, I'm just not up to it."

"Hey, we don't have to go. But that's not like you. Are you okay?" Bo waited for her response, but none came. "Babe. What is it? Why the sad eyes?"

As if that were a cue for the waterworks, Margret crumpled into herself, becoming a mass of snot and tears. "Bo, I want to adopt a baby."

This proclamation came out of the sheer blue. From a different planet.

"You get home from this conference and meet your idol of all times, and this is the takeaway? What am I not getting?"

Bo immediately realized how insensitive he sounded. His wife was inconsolable, which was very rare for her. What now? Maybe an apology and a cup of tea?

Margret swiped her nose with a handful of tissues. She wasn't angry and realized how out of character it seemed for her to be sobbing. How could he know what triggered this, or why it had erupted without warning?

"I love you so much, Bo." That was not an explanation.

Bo put his arm around her. "Love you too, baby. But how did you go from making professional connections and growing your career to wanting to stay home and raise somebody else's baby?"

She let out a stuttering sigh. Emotion coursed through her lymphatic system. She even let the 'someone else's baby' comment pass. He was probably shocked by the mention of having a baby to think it through, that an adopted child would be theirs in every respect but biological.

"I looked around at this incredible hi-tech auditorium with an amazing sound system and seating better than any deluxe movie theater. And yes, August Jamison was incredible." Maybe in a dusty corner of her brain she had a tiny schoolgirl crush on him, and had she not just learned about Bo's unusual experience at the theater, she might have sought the great Jamison out after his presentation and introduced herself, hoping for a shred of conversation, which would then go no further. It's a mystery why we seek validation from strangers, she mused.

"What happened?" Bo asked.

Margret balled up her tissues and lofted them into the garbage can by the kitchen sink, smiling through a veil of tears. "I saw women like me. Hundreds of them. All suited up, looking very corporate and listening so intently, nodding and smiling at the right times. They were all planning the next move in their careers. And here I was, tuning out."

"Even to the great August Jamison?"

She smiled. "Yup. Well, after the first five minutes. I was at rapt attention at first."

Bo poked her.

Margret continued. "I was so worried about your frame of mind after seeing the play and then suddenly my mind drifted. For some reason, this scene came into my head. I was standing over a changing station with a tiny infant looking up at me. She had the biggest brown eyes I ever saw and she was smiling at me. I don't know where it popped up from, but I realized that all this," she motioned to her suitcase in the hallway, the textbooks in the bookcase, "being caught up in my career, was meant to be put aside. Now is that time."

Margret and Bo had already been through the disappointment of trying to have a baby with no results. After three years, Bo agreed to get tested. He found out his sperm were robust and ready.

Margret, on the other hand, had uncooperative fallopian tubes. Even if in vitro were a possibility, they couldn't meet the expense. They had discussed a surrogate for about five minutes before agreeing it wasn't for them.

The only other options were 1) to adopt, or 2) live as they were, happily, as a childless couple.

Bo had slowly accepted the idea of being together in perpetuity without progeny. Things were great, they were in love, their careers were going places. Initially Margret thought she was on board.

She wheeled her luggage into the bedroom and turned to him. Her fingers traced the geometric patterns in the bedspread. "This conference was just great, Bo. You should have heard them talking about the new technologies. It's so exciting!"

"If I'm hearing you right, you want to put all that on hold?" he asked.

She nodded and squeezed out a few more tears.

CHAPTER 21

The melody that Gramma Ida taught Bo and his cousins was a simple round like "Row Your Boat," but it had the effect of a bird warbling its heart out in pure avian joy. It began with three high, trilled notes followed by a sudden dip more than an octave lower, repeating several times for a total of 24 beats. Lymus had some crazy imagination, thought Bo, in defying the conventions of predictable phrasing. It was even more amazing considering that the only music his great-great uncle could have heard were etudes and classical music, nothing breaking the formulaic compositions of the time.

Scandals of Violet featured catchy Broadway-worthy music, but it was the main melody from the song "My Heart has Feathers Aloft," repeated in various permutations during the play's nearly two hours, that had shocked Bo's soul and now implored him to take action; what that would look like, he didn't yet know.

The warbling lilt and interval jumps in "My Heart" were unmistakably lifted from Lymus's song, of that Bo was sure. The lyrics that Gramma had passed down had uncannily fit the cadence of Fetterman's song, snapping into place like an enormous puzzle piece. What drove it all home for him was the bluesy way the lead male sang it. It brought Lymus to life and water to Bo's eyes.

I need to channel this. I need to make something from this and dedicate it to Lymus. What if he wrote his own song based on Lymus's melody? Bo could easily imagine a sax bending the hell out of the notes and slathering on a wide, fat vibrato on top. What this really amounted to was negating Fetterman's work and re-inventing it Bo's way, first with a heavy hand then gradually tapering off with delicacy and respect for its originator.

Bo wanted the bass to make the opening musical statement. Not many songs started with the bass establishing the melody rather than its typical role laying down rhythm. The music that did this successfully made a unique impact on the listener. The song would then be tossed around like a beach ball to piano and sax. But how and when would this music see the light of day? Who was going to hear this song, and who would play it?

Those details would come later. For now, it was all about sketching out the song. Bo let his mind wander. What if we got the old gang together and played some original music? He composed a song with his former band members in mind: Joey Fritz on drums, Tim McKnight on piano and Pip Jones on sax.

After the bass's dominating entrance, percussion would hit it, approaching lightly at first with a little high hat and mostly brushes, then gradually driving the motif home with ten assertive single beats, the snare tuned up a fifth to reinforce the uplifting nature of the song. Joey would make the sticks dance (if he could even find Joey; that was a different question entirely). Add his hysterical friend Pip Jones on sax and the cool and collected Tim McKnight on piano...everybody all in, so long as Bo could find them.

The end of the song would then return to its opening bird-like warble, only to conclude without melodic resolution – because life was not that pat – not on the leading seventh nor the root nor its fifth, but with a second that trailed off into the ether. The last instrument to be heard would be the sax, which would have the final musical say with three soft, high notes into a fade-out.

Bo wrote as much as he could before even thinking about edits, about performing it or if it would ever be heard. It didn't matter.

He called it "Lines for Lymus."

CHAPTER 22

"Listen, you really want to bust open this thing with Lymus's music, maybe you should bone up on Dexie Abbott." Margret was referring to a more recent rung on Bo's family tree.

"The only thing I want to bone up on is you!"

Bo rolled on his side, towards Margret, and gently swung his leg over her. An unexpectedly deep kiss followed.

Margret was never one to turn away affection unless she was getting ready for work. Being Saturday, there was nothing she'd rather do than spend some time getting hot and heavy.

After 14 years of marriage he still tasted delicious, like spiced caramel. His smooth skin and muscular legs were still a huge turn-on.

The conversation about his forebears was put on hold as Bo's desire grew. He pressed into Margret. She matched him move for move. Maybe they would make a baby, she thought.

Bo was an expert at knowing where she needed the most attention, how she wanted him to move and at what pace. He was all over her with his tongue, hands and legs. She mimicked his urgency and brought him what he needed.

When they were done, Bo exhaled loudly, then chuckled.

"What's so funny?" asked a mellow and satisfied Margret.

"It's just that I make this bad pun about boning you, and it turns you on."

It wasn't his adolescent humor that got her going. It was that his desire stayed strong no matter what they were going through. This kept the flame alive year after year. May it be so forever.

She turned to her side and fit her head into his warm armpit. "Really, though," she resumed, "if you do some sleuthing, maybe you can find more tidbits that lead back to Lymus. You never know."

"You could have a point. There's a lot about Fetterman that I need to look into. I don't know how he came to be in the same orbit as Lymus, but there's a connection somehow. There has to be." Bo stretched, gently rolling her away so he could get up. "But now I'm ready for a nice hot shower with that peppermint body wash you got at the farmer's market. Join me?"

"Why not?" she lobbed. Maybe it would lead to round two.

Early on in their relationship, the baggage they carried with them had caused a bit of power posturing and in a few instances led to some hellacious fights about trust and boundaries. Margret's issues had scalded her and she found herself acting out the harsh treatment she received as a young girl from an alcoholic mother. Therapy helped bring this to light and Margret was able to let go of the demons, treat herself better and not lash out at her husband.

Bo had a wholesome upbringing so there were no problems in his formative years. He went through the typical angry phase as a teenager where everything was an uphill fight. He'd mellowed out by the time he hit 21, but the toxic feelings came pouring back one year later when the "love of his life" broke off their engagement. He was most upset at himself for being vulnerable. It took a while to trust things with Margret and realize that she was another person altogether.

She had even walked out once, ending up on the subway until she reached her friend Betsy's house at the other end of Brooklyn, where she remained for the night. Betsy was smart enough not to tear Bo to shreds, since from all indications Margret and Bo were the real McCoy and they belonged together.

The time apart scared both of them and made them realize that maintaining a combative stance wasn't sustainable for a healthy marriage. It was also exhausting. Like any couple, there were destined to be occasional frustrations as they continued to write their marital choreography. That was where music came in. It was Bo's salve. Margaret relied on her friends.

The Midtown Manhattan library beckoned to Bo. He unearthed a spiral notebook from his music room-slash-office and set out for an afternoon alone as a wandering researcher. The cathedral of books was a great place to start. Even if the library didn't produce any new information, the atmosphere was inspiring. He'd make sure to visit the sound archives to hear rare recordings of early 1900s jazz. Now that would be a treat.

"I'm going to visit the lions," he said, remembering the statues' place in their history together. It was there, in front of the library 15 years ago, that they had both played hooky (he worked as a tech in Radiology and she was pursuing a Master's in Public Health) to spend the day in the city. When they emerged from the subway, both high on life, high on each other, it felt as if they had walked right into the morning sun, blinded by an immense light that filled their view. When they turned around to climb the library steps stretching out in front of them, Margret had no idea he'd fall to one knee in front of the iconic lions and ask his question. When she said yes, Bo knew he had the best reason in the world to lie to his boss that day.

CHAPTER 23

Bo was starting to become obsessed with "Lines for Lymus," but the song clearly needed a reason to exist, and to have an impact on the world (or whoever would listen to it), it needed a vehicle carrying it out into the open.

Making this dream a reality required a lot of digging in and facing what he had meekly avoided his whole musical life, which was to compose and release his own CD.

He allowed the thought to linger awhile before taking any action. The state of suspension prior to making a concrete plan was daunting and thrilling at the same time. The only thing holding him back was confidence, which, curiously, wasn't lacking in his career and other aspects of his life, just with music.

The guys he used to gig with, if he could call it that (it was more that they filled a half hour here and there at the local watering holes, often with no compensation other than beer on tap), could be living anywhere in the world, and even if he could find them, they might not be receptive to a musical reunion. With the exception of Pip Jones (now a college band director in Boston) whom Bo had stayed in touch with, he had no idea what the other two guys were up to.

Assuming they were into it, this wasn't just going to be a one-time, happy-go-lucky reunion. It was a commitment. It'd put him deep in the tangled woods of inventing, coordinating, pushing and motivating. When he was 22, all he had to do was think about writing songs and he'd be met with an endless stream of ideas. Sticky notes littered his bulletin board, his desk, the case of his bass. Since he started his "real" career (it pained him to call it that) at the hospital when he was 23, the ideas slowed to a trickle. Maybe the creativity was there, but it had been pushed down deep in his fear center. Healthcare was much more accessible and paid the bills. He wasn't sure he could say the same about music.

Margret didn't agree. She always told him to follow his heart, and she was far from the pie-in-the-sky dreamer of the family. From the time she earned her MPH and moved into administration at the hospital, she earned a respectable salary. More than anything, she wanted to hand him his dreams on a shiny silver platter. As the years wore on, any talk of his pursuing music slipped quietly away.

One morning when they were getting ready for work, Bo told her about the song he was writing. "I feel an opus coming on." Mags looked at him quizzically. He stood near the dresser, shirtless, tying the drawstrings of his scrub pants.

"After seeing *Scandals* and working on the song about Lymus, I think I want to make music that honors him and all the creatives from that era who will never have their time in the sun." Just saying it made him feel sad and powerful at the same time.

"A CD? That's pretty cool. How would that happen, exactly?"

"Good question. One song at a time. I have all these melodies and time signatures floating around in my head, and I've been thinking about how to attack the main problem."

Margret divided her hair into three silky ropes to twist into a braid. She'd wanted to cut her hair many times, but it defined her vision of femininity. "What problem?"

"Personnel."

"Go on?"

Bo grinned at her. "You think the Fab Four can be revived?"

"You mean Pip and the other two, what were their names?" she asked.

"Joey and Tim. Why not? It's certainly worth a phone call. I'm not getting any younger, and one day we won't be able to play together anymore. I just want to experience that magic again, and this time with real meaning behind it."

"It always had meaning, Bo," she said. "But I get that this is on a different level. Whatever makes you happy makes me happy." She stepped over to him and lightly played with his chest hair. It was dark and curly with hints of gray. *This is very sexy,* she thought.

Bo caught her vibe and smiled. "I first have to see if the guys would be into it. I'd want all four of us, because I know how we can lay it down, but I also feel that it can be scalable if one of them isn't interested or they don't return my calls. I'd just have to know who's in, so I can write for it."

The thought of the guys not jumping at the chance to work on something new and exciting – typically an irresistible challenge for any jazz musician worth his salt – made Margret wistful. The reality was that it might not happen. In the worst-case scenario, would he make a CD by himself?

Regardless of whether the other musicians were available, it was a personal journey that Bo felt compelled to take, bringing him face to face with his painful ancestry.

CHAPTER 24

Doubt was beginning to nibble away at Bo and it was relentless.

So many things could go wrong. Making a CD was a huge undertaking and would eat up most of a year in writing and production. If it ever got finished, it could turn out to be a mere proton blip in music history. Aside from the eventual release party when the CD was complete, it was very likely there'd be no further impact on anyone, ever again. The guys would continue in their lives and careers, and nobody would think about the songs inspired by the long-gone Lymus Abbott. Nobody would know of his struggles, what inspired him, what kept the light on.

If you create art but no one notices, does it really happen? Is it still art at that point or just an empty passage of time?

These were Bo's thoughts every morning for a week as he transitioned from sleep to wakefulness, those moments when you try to grab onto your dreams for a clearer recollection but they slip away like sand.

"Sounds to me a little like inertia with a dollop of depression," Margret observed as she lay next to Bo. It was 5 a.m. on a Friday. The weekend tantalized them from a distance. "If you're passionate about this, you need to shut those negative thoughts off. You know that's all they are."

Bo lifted his head slightly and reached behind to flip his pillow. "I feel like this is an undoable project. There are so many moving parts that depend on other people."

"You have to figure out how much you love the project, and if you do, you need to love the process, or build a process that you love. Otherwise you'll resent the whole thing."

Margret was right. Nobody was holding a gun to his head to do this. He could finish "Lines for Lymus" as a bass solo, even add some backing tracks he could buy online, and put it up on YouTube and voilà: original music available to the masses. No cost, no hassle, no depending on other people. If he wanted to get back to playing, he could re-connect with the musicians from the night at the Met.

And yet, he didn't have to do any of that. He could ditch the project completely and just go out to hear live jazz whenever the mood struck. Or put on a record or a CD or stay in bed forever with the blanket pulled over his head...

"When I think of what I want to achieve, it's giving form to Lymus through music. I don't want to turn my back on that. I can't unhear the song from *Scandals* and I can't invalidate what my Gramma sang to me." Bo huffed and Margret reached out for his hand.

"I know," she said softly. "Eat the elephant one bite at a time. It's the only way. You'll get there. If you need some tension release, I'm always here right next to ya." She squeezed his hand.

There was only one way to approach this mountainous challenge: clear a path in his mind and push his way through.

And make some damn calls.

CHAPTER 25

"We are from the same tribe," Margret stated flatly. "I mean, way back." It was a Sunday New York Times kind of day. Pajamas ruled.

Bo chuckled, but took exception to her statement. "I don't think so, babes. My dad's people came from Africa many moons ago...and on my mother's side, the tribes of Judea, if you want to get technical."

A smile spread over Margret's face. Talking about their backgrounds made her feel good. She loved that their ancestors had come from different corners of the globe and would never have met, let alone fallen in love. Yet here they were, in the soft amber cast of their bedroom, cuddled together on a luscious king-sized bed. As it always was, each half completed the other. This was the inner sanctum.

"And," Bo added, "your people are from clans. So there!"

"Not *the* Klan," she protested, then giggled.

"Clans, like with the tartan plaids and all that. Right?"

"I love a man with a kilt. You ought to try it sometime."

There was silence. Neither one moved. Each was wondering whether the moment would get intimate. They might have been too tired.

Bo tried his best. "Come here, you sassy lassie."

"Oh, you want to play that? Okay, my hot brotha," she responded. Then she frowned. "Eh, never mind. That's too familial. Sorry, I lost it, sweetie."

When all else failed, there was always ice cream. Bo got the rocky road from the freezer, shoved two spoons into the virgin pint and returned to his bride.

"Now, we're talking," Margret said, appreciatively prying off a spoonful.

She sucked off a mound of ice cream and handed the carton back to him. "I only wanted a little taste," she said. "So hon. You know how I love Max Fleisher, right?"

"Yeah, the guy who drew Felix the Cat?" Bo said.

"Exactly. Well, for one of my college electives, I took film studies. There was a lot of creativity in the early cartoons, especially from Fleischer, and it had more social commentary than people realize."

"I guess," mused Bo. "Do you recall any references to jazz? That would be interesting."

"Yeah. I was looking for the social caricatures of the times, like how blacks and Jews were portrayed. The Irish and Italians too, they were down there in the social strata. Jazz definitely had an influence in the cartoon world. I seem to remember some short animation about Louis Armstrong and Cab Calloway."

"Pretty cool," said Bo. "We actually played some Calloway at the party I did at the Met. Maybe we should look some of this stuff up on YouTube."

"Okay," she said. "Pull out your laptop. Let's take a look."

"First things first. Something I want to check out." Bo started searching 'scandals of' and immediately three videos popped up.

"Try the first one," she said, pointing to an image of a record with the label *Okeh*.

"Look at this," said Bo. "The description says '*Scandals* was written by two cousins who called themselves Elsner and Price, but their original names were Ellerdorff and Pinckus. German Jews who wanted to sound more Americanized.'"

"Never heard of them," said Margret.

"I know, right? Here it goes on to say they panicked and tried to quash the musical right after it came out because of pressure from Tin Pan Alley, which favored the Gershwins, but it stayed in production for another year after *Porgy and Bess*."

Margret was reading further down the page. "You were not kidding."

"About what?" he asked.

"About Fetterman. He's your guy."

The last paragraph stated:

Possibly the driving force in keeping "Scandals of Violet" alive for another 12 months was due to the determined first-time producer from the north Bronx, Bernard Jerome Fetterman, who with his wife Lottie, put all their money into what they felt was a 'sure thing'.

"Let's play this baby already," said Bo.

They sat in silence as Lymus's song about a mama bird played on the scratchy recording. The trumpet sailed into the sky and the vocals followed.

"And so now you see." His heart pounded. He still wasn't used to the feeling of shock.

"What now?" she asked.

"Well, it says underneath the video that the record is courtesy of the Smithsonian Museum. I say we make a trip there," Bo suggested.

"You know I don't have any vacation time." Margret was getting anxious. "Do you really want to take the time to chase this down?"

Bo shook his head. "Babe."

"What?"

"Yes, I really do. Can't you see it's important to me?"

Margret saw that, but she also saw the man she loved in pain. "Honey, go there if you want. Please just come back to me, and I mean mentally, too."

"I will. That guy Fetterman, he's an evil dude. I don't care that he has all these friends and that he gave me a free ticket to his play. He and his wife stole the music, or took stolen music from somebody else, and made it their own. I'm trying to figure this out. Nothing makes sense."

"Well, did you talk to Zack?" she asked.

Bo told her about their conversation and that Zack wasn't too hopeful of finding a good resolution, but he'd try.

"I think this is a pattern. Historically speaking," he said.

Margret weighed her words and decided to say what was on her mind. "The next thing you're going to tell me is that Jews control the music industry."

Bo reached for her hand. "I'm not...I just don't know what to think."

"Really, Bo?" she asked. "Your mom's people, infiltrating every aspect of composition, performance, production, PR and whatnot? That's just not true. Where are all the supposed high-profile entertainment people in your mother's family, then? I haven't heard a word about that in all the time I've known you." Margret released his hand and crossed her arms. She hated stereotypes.

"No," Bo said slowly. "I guess that sounds like an exaggeration. But in this case, let's be real, in the 20s and 30s, before we all intermarried, it could have been very close to the truth." He saw her posture relax.

Bo continued. "I read everything I could find on our favorite husband-wife troupe, that dear duo, aka 'The Fettermans.' The press made no bones about how influential they were. People tolerated him, yeah, but they absolutely trembled at the thought of her. I still think that's the case, even if they're ancient."

Margret fluffed up her pillows. "Book your trip but please don't stay long. Maybe you'll find some resolution," she said, rubbing his arm. "Anyway, I've seen enough YouTube for now. Hand me the book review?"

Bo cracked open his laptop again. According to the Smithsonian's website, they had a Civil War museum with nearly a thousand photos, many of them located in the building's archives. He pored over about two hundred of them. Several appeared to be sheet music, but the images were part of a larger collage and impossible to zoom in without losing the details.

He'd call them the next day and ask to meet with the director as soon as there was an opening, explaining that he was researching his family lineage and his particular interest in the sheet music. Bo's goal was to get a much closer look at all the sheet music they had.

It was all set. He was going to DC, with or without vacation pay, just as soon as he could confirm a meeting with the top guy. Maybe the trip would throw some light on the situation, discrediting his fears about the provenance of the music and putting his suspicions to rest. Or it could lead to something more disturbing. Either way, he had to find out.

CHAPTER 26

Margret sent Bo on his way via cab to Newark International Airport on a Sunday night. He brought a small carry-on with his laptop. In his wallet was the ticket stub to *Scandals*.

He had arranged coverage in the ER from a colleague named Jenna who worked in Marketing. She had started at County Memorial in registration a decade ago, making her the perfect sub for the day. The department was on auto-pilot anyway, so there were no worries. He wondered if Aimee would be put off by Jenna's presence, since Jenna had a vibrant demeanor that commanded interaction. In marketing, that was a plus. With a jealous woman around, not so much.

The flight would be short and the hotel room proved to be a quick cab ride away.

When he arrived, he carded his way into the room and collapsed on the bed. It was an emotional journey; all of it.

The next morning, he woke up early from the excitement.

After a disappointing hotel breakfast and a scorching roast coffee from a trendy place up the street, he walked over to the Civil War Museum, a brick porticoed building, and found the rooms devoted to slave life. He had a lot of time to spend before his four o'clock appointment with the director.

The exhibit was, to say the least, disconcerting. He was struck by the contrast between a matter-of-fact, perhaps even joyous, Uncle Remus-type existence with artfully constructed dioramas hiding the tragic reality that robbed his ancestors and so many others of their freedom and basic human dignity. Its unapologetic nature shouldn't have been surprising but it made him gasp.

In one of the cases was a huge thatch of the grasses which slaves wove together "in their free time" to create items for everyday use. *Seriously, their 'free' time?* Bo wondered. *Nothing about their life was free. Jesus!*

With skillful hands and from a humble vegetative beginning, they created objects like baskets, placemats, picture frames, pedestals and door mats, many of which now existed only as fragments. It proved that no matter the circumstances, hope is always present. That it manifested itself in art remained one of the constant truths of humankind's time on earth.

At first glance, if you were just walking by quickly, it could seem like the items were local artifacts that had a pleasing but uninteresting sameness. A closer look revealed each had been imaginatively crafted with complicated patterns that seemed almost impossible to represent with just pieces of grass. Platters and wall hangings illustrated the phases of the moon, a sunset, field workers and farmers. Others had birds and snakes, hearts, geometric patterns, even a surprising foray into portraiture. Bo admired the artists' ingenuity. It must have tested their faith every minute to live as they did, diminished, yet still be hopeful. Bo bowed his head and said a prayer for them. He couldn't imagine the harrowing realities they faced every minute of their lives.

The exhibit had acrylic cases placed randomly where other smaller items were displayed. He saw trays of wooden beads, some still strung; purses; knives and forks carved from bones; and a variety of blue-cast pottery. He wondered where the blue color came from. Was it a berry? The placard indicated it was from the indigo plants that grew wild. What a gorgeous hue, he thought to himself. Beauty all around us, hiding in plain sight.

Next to this exhibit was paper ephemera: recipes, worn postcards that the plantation owners and their families had discarded but which were salvaged for their beautiful (and at the time, exceedingly new) photographic images: scenes of sizeable trees, stately homes with wide columns and spacious wraparound porches, flooded rice paddies, birds and alligators under wooden bridges. A display case on a nearby pedestal held a carved oaken box with a vine design that caught his eye. It was similar to a medallion he had seen in his Gramma's breakfront. The box didn't have a medallion, and that was the stunner, because there was an unvarnished oval where something obviously had once been but had now fallen off.

The next room held more paper artifacts: news leaflets, drawings and the like. Suddenly, his feet were fused to the floor. He stared at the papers behind the thick plexiglass. There, at the bottom of the exhibit, was the sheet music that had caught his eye online and had prompted his call to the director's office.

The writing was barely legible. It looked as if the ink had run off from years of dirt and water damage. He could read a few letters and maybe a word here and there, but the primitive musical notation was unmistakable. Whoever wrote it had an uncanny grasp of music theory even though the method he used to notate it was unconventional. For example, instead of five lines on the musical staff, there were four. Instead of circles for the notes the composer used an X. Still, Bo understood the composer's intentions.

He wondered if he was looking at Lymus's work as he stared into the case. He caught his own reflection staring back at him and noticed his mouth was open.

Bo needed a break. Outside, food trucks lined the boulevard. He found a vendor selling soul food and got a heaping plate of rice, beans and collard greens that tasted like his Gramma's cooking. Four p.m. couldn't come quickly enough. He filled the rest of the time with a walk through the downtown area and wandered into a music store where he bought a set of strings for his bass.

Finally, it was time to meet the director. Bo found his way to the over-designed administrative office surrounded by Persian tapestries on one side and monochromatic modern art on the other. Every desk was its own statement; some had classic roll-tops with ornate woodwork and others were clever 1960s chrome-legged jobs topped with marbled Formica. The inner office where he would meet with Roy Stokes, Head of Acquisitions, was barely visible from the reception area, down the end of a hallway to the left.

His nerves on edge, he knew he was either on the precipice of a remarkable revelation or soon to receive the most daunting disappointment imaginable, in either case without Margret there to share it. This would force him to confront the truth, even at its worst, without the buffer of her presence. He would soon find out if he was unbreakable...whatever the outcome.

Temples pulsing wildly, Bo found a Charlie Parker tune to set his anxiety to: "Now's the Time." With its locked-in rhythm, Parker's flawless attack on the sax and perfect complement by piano provided the right frame of mind. Bo unclenched his jaw, took a deep breath, and exhaled slowly. *Just go with it. How bad could it be?*

The door opened and into the receptionist's area strode a tall, fit man who could probably be considered attractive in a gentle, unflappable way. He set his impossibly pale blue eyes on Bo and lanked his way over, wearing a lopsided smile that Bo hoped wasn't his patronizing look. Margret had told him many times that he had a tendency to catastrophize before he had enough information to make a sane judgment. *OK Mags, I'm hearing you. Easy does it.*

"A fond hello, Mr. Abbott." Stokes's voice was deep and his tone was direct. He stretched out a long-fingered hand. This man could easily be a bassist. Bo obliged and found the handshake to be surprisingly non-assertive. Maybe there was hope, Bo mused, immediately berating himself for assessing this individual on irrelevant details.

"Please, come this way. How was your flight?"

Chit-chat may be a good sign. *Stop overanalyzing everything that comes out of his mouth.* It will either be good news or not. Regardless, there would be a flight back home with Margret waiting for him, a return to the mundanities of work, and life would go on.

"The plane was smooth and quick. Couldn't ask for more," Bo answered. He tried to lighten his tone but he was still on edge, and with the rice and beans, now he was also uncomfortably full.

"I'm happy to be here," he added. It was a half-truth. The dread had resurfaced and with it came palpitations that he swore could be seen through his white linen dress shirt.

There was too much art in Stokes's office and Bo had no idea where to look. The pressure in his temples started dancing again, and Charlie Parker didn't help quell it.

"So Mr. Abbott –" the tall man began.

"Bo, please."

"Of course; Bo. I know this is very important to you, otherwise you wouldn't have requested a meeting on such short notice." Stokes scratched his arm above a neatly rolled shirtsleeve. He was casual and fastidious at the same time, and his smile seemed genuine.

Bo sat down on the edge of a chair and fidgeted. "My apologies, I hope I didn't put you out."

A melodic laugh immediately lightened the mood. "Not at all," Stokes chimed. "I'm intrigued! Let me tell you my findings and then we can discuss where to go from here. In essence –"

Crud. Here it comes.

"I know what you are looking for, but we can't give you an answer."

Bo deflated. He thought this would be a binary situation. He didn't count on being no better off, no worse off than he was seven minutes ago.

"It's just that we can't assure the provenance of many of the items here. I can, however, tell you how we came to receive that sheet music. Luckily for us, the gifting information is unclassified per the donor's agreement. The Raynor family of Charleston found these sheaves of paper, but nobody knows exactly who wrote them."

"I see." He sat up straighter. "Can I examine them closer for signatures or other markings?"

"I've expected you might ask me that," said Stokes. Bo thought he was winning him over. Thank God.

"I've already made arrangements for you to see the head curator and view these documents in our research laboratory," the tall man continued. "You'll have to wear goggles and gloves, and the lighting is a very bright blue. I think you'll like it. Did you ever want to be an astronaut?"

Bo smiled at this attempt at humor. "Thank you, Mr. Stokes, I would enjoy that very much."

"It's Roy. And please relax, we're happy to have somebody who shows such an interest in these artifacts. My grandmother was the daughter of a slave – yes, I know I'm quite light, but nevertheless – and it's a topic near and dear to my heart. Good luck, Bo, and please follow me."

CHAPTER 27

At eight p.m., Bo's cab let him off at his front door. It had been a difficult weekend.

Margret was watching the news when he came in. She shut it off and jumped up to kiss him, taking his luggage from him and wheeling it into the hallway.

Bo headed into the bathroom for a long, steamy shower and left the door open. She came in and sat on the closed toilet seat. "Are you okay?"

A cloud of heat billowed around him, hiding his face. He rubbed the shower door clear so he could see her. "I can't shake what I saw at the exhibit, and then afterwards in the lab. It felt like Lymus was there in the room with me, looking over my shoulder."

"What happened?"

"It was like wearing a HazMat suit and being in quarantine. Very clinical and futuristic."

"What about the sheet music?"

"The music could have been totally unrelated to the song about the bird. But there was a scribble at the bottom, and to me, the initials looked like 'LJA'. I can't be sure, and I called Stokes over and he said it might be but he wasn't sure either. I'll show you on my phone, but it came out with weird lighting because I had to keep the flash off."

Margret had brought in a cup of chamomile tea. Bo was lathering up with bergamot and patchouli soap and it smelled amazing.

"He said I could contact the donors. Maybe they'd know what's written on it. He gave me their info. Not so sure I want to reach out to them, though."

"Why not?" she asked.

"Maybe I'm afraid of what I might find. What if they're descended from the plantation owner? Why would I want to meet somebody like that?"

It was a very serious thing to wrap their heads around.

"Well, you could talk to them and see where it takes you," she said. "The more you learn about it, the better your ability to process this."

"At this point, I want to do more than talk. I think those artifacts belong to us, and when I say us, I mean our family. My pops, for example, and his brother and sister."

Margret had no idea whether something like sheet music could be repatriated. "Do you want it taken out of the exhibit? It's really beautiful, its history and hopefulness. I just wonder if it will inspire people who see it."

Bo wanted to stay in the shower forever. "How would you feel? Wouldn't you want something like this back home with you?" he asked.

"I actually have no idea," she responded. "I suppose so. You might have a huge battle in front of you, though."

"I know. And sorry if I snapped at you. It's been an emotional couple of days for me."

She smiled and blew him a kiss. "I know. You didn't snap. It's such an unbelievable situation. Whatever you decide, I'm here with you."

"Also, and I'm too tired to get into it right now, but there was a carved wooden box with a missing piece that looked just like that medallion you've seen at Gramma's house. I think my cousin Freddy was going to give that to me a while back after she died. I'm going to ask him about it." He turned off the water and she handed him a towel.

Bo wondered if the items were permanent fixtures at the museum or if they would eventually be cycled back to a storage room to make way for another exhibit.

"I just want you to be prepared to hit a brick wall," she added. "We don't know for a fact that Lymus Abbott wrote the notes and lyrics on those sheets. The Smithsonian as the holding company could very well say nothing more we can do, so sorry, and bye."

His inner core told him that these had Abbott lineage. Their origins sat somewhere on a branch of his family tree.

"Really, there's just one thing I want above all. I want Lymus to get his due. His day in the sun. How to achieve this, I've still got to figure out, but stay tuned."

"I'm not going anywhere."

CHAPTER 28

"These guys did a complete 180 flip on my great-great uncle Lymus. It's unconscionable."

Margret searched Bo's face. "Did something new come up?"

It was a Wednesday evening and they'd both finished off a pot of well-seasoned coq au vin. They sat in their living room flipping through shows to watch on cable.

Bo drew in a breath, then let it out with a groan. "I can't believe I'm saying this, but these rich white guys out-and-out stole my family's work."

Margret frowned. She'd seen him ping-pong between acceptance and frustration, and at the moment he was reeling at what he called the 'Broadway machine.'

"Zack said he can't prove anything was specifically stolen," she said. "I agree with you, the songs sound completely the same to me. But Zack was pretty clear that the statute has long passed, and even still, it's just too thin a case to win."

Bo replayed the image of sitting in the theater, immobile, with the orchestra seeping into his ears. How he forgot to breathe. Super-glued in place, impotent; stoic on the outside with a pool of hot bubbling panic beneath.

"I know it's over a week already, but I still feel powerless. It's driving me crazy." He punched a pillow.

Margret muted the remote. "Are you going to pursue having the sheet music returned to the Abbots?"

"No," said Bo. "It's much better being out in the open so people can view it. I might want to talk to them about adding more information to the placard. But that's something for another day." He rubbed his face. "It's all so exhausting."

"What about going for a walk?" she suggested. "It's not dark yet and we can stretch our legs. Come on, get your jacket on." Margret saw him get up and open the hall closet. That was a good sign.

Of all the things they did together, their long walks were the simplest and the most enjoyable. They talked things through, analyzed their feelings, let their guards down and strengthened the bond between them. They laughed, joked, poked fun at their problems and worked through their issues.

Bo needed that now more than anything else. His struggle to process his family's past and the responsibility to make things right was just starting.

CHAPTER 29

Dear Mr. Fetterman,

I just saw The Scandals of Violet and wanted first to thank you for the ticket! You may recall you met me at the Met. I was the bassist you said reminded you of Charlie Mingus.

I wanted to congratulate you and Mrs. Fetterman, and of course the cast and crew for a job well done. What an amazing evening! As a musician, I especially enjoyed the score. It was off the charts (pun intended)!

Bo's enthusiasm was mixed with an ulterior motive. He wanted to butter him up before laying a big fat goose egg, a card that would be played later. He continued:

I've not gotten many gigs since my college days but the Met was a great time, Bo continued. *Nowadays I make a living in healthcare. But I wanted to speak to you about something of personal interest concerning the music in your play. Could you fit me in for a quick cup of coffee somewhere in the city, at your convenience?*

With warm regards,
Bo Sonski-Abbott

Bo hoped the old guy would get to read his message, not just an underpaid assistant who instantly deleted everything after reading it. Would this raise a red flag as to his true intentions, an exploratory of intellectual property issues? Maybe he was being paranoid. Hopefully Fetterman would take it as an innocuous note of appreciation. From the way the producer treated his posse of colleagues, he relied on his fans for validation even while disdaining them.

There was a shred of a chance that the old vaudevillian (vaude*villain?* mused Bo) would accept an offer for a quick cup since, for some reason, he had seemed to like Bo. You never know unless you ask, thought Bo. He hit 'send.'

That precise instant in time when you regret releasing an email? Bo's stomach clenched. *Oh crap, now his people are going to look at my social media to see if I'm a kook.* Bo quickly checked his Facebook and Twitter feeds. All good. Nothing political or controversial except for some armchair activism about school funding for the arts. It was all true to form, about jazz and food and the subways.

He had allowed some time to pass before reaching out to Fetterman, and now was a good time to face what might happen next: confrontation or friendly conversation?

"Screw it," he told Margret. "What's the worst that can happen?"

CHAPTER 30

The email in his inbox glowed invitingly.

By hovering over the sender's email address, it seemed to be legit, indicating it was from BF@BFETTERMANENTERPRISES.com. Bernie's profile picture showed him in his much younger days, wearing a tux at some big-deal award night. His heart doing a rhumba, Bo clicked on the message.

Dear Bo,

Thank you so much for your kind words. Lottie and I enjoyed putting this little show together. I am hopeful for it to be my swan song into retirement, which I've promised and reneged on too many times to count, but is definitely imminent. HAHA.

I have a 10am meeting at the BMI offices at 7 World Trade Center next Thursday morning. If you want to be in the reception area at 9:30, there's a few chairs around and we can chat. That's about the only time I have available.

Regards.
BF

Bo had been holding his breath. He let it out and slammed his palm on the desk. "Mags!"

"What is it?" She walked into their office with a handful of bills fanned out. Her glasses sat crookedly on her nose. No matter how much adjusting she did, she always looked off-kilter with her specs on. She was very cute.

"He said yes! I'm going to have a few minutes with Bernie Fetterman. The great, the mysterious, the--- well, let me reserve judgment."

"That's just fabulous." She smiled, but her words came out lukewarm. Bo wasn't sure why that would be.

"It's the only chance to get a feel for my...dilemma, you know?" he asked.

The situation wasn't exactly a dilemma.

"I know you said you were going to do this," she said, measuring her words. "But now that he said he'll meet you, what are you going to say without looking like you're asking for compensation?"

His gaze jumped from her left eye to her right eye, and how her glasses just wouldn't sit level no matter what. Maybe her ears were not on the same plane?

"I don't think that's an issue. My strategy is to sing his praises. Tell him how relatable the music was, how enjoyable the production was. Then talk about my upcoming CD. And then I guess launch into Lymus's music. I can show him the photo I took at the Civil War Museum."

"And what's your ask? The guy only has like fifteen minutes at most. You have to get to the point pretty quickly."

"Right. I need to present myself so he at least listens."

Margret was puzzled. It wouldn't be a happy meeting once the name Lymus was mentioned. Why did Bo seem so excited?

"What I want to ask him is to put one of those addendums they slip into the Playbill, like when they have a change in the cast, to say something like 'credit for *My Heart Has Feathers to Fly* is attributed to the memory of Lymus Abbott'."

One sentence of acknowledgement would be huge; it would be everything. It would set the record straight.

"I'd even sign a no-sue or release-from-harm contract if he wanted. If he's ever asked about it by the press, he can just say it was somebody that his friend knew long ago. Or he doesn't have to say anything."

Margret's heart didn't have feathers and it wasn't flying, but it sure was pounding. This could go sideways in a snap. Legal intervention was needed before things got any further.

"Bo, do me a favor. Please run this by Zack?"

It felt like she threw a bucket of cold water on a nice toasty fire, but he knew she was right. "I get your point. I already sent the email, so I'll have to tell Fetterman something else over coffee in the event Zack tells me to back off."

It was a good thing he listened to reason. No doubt Bernard Fetterman had a huge legion of attorneys just waiting to pounce on anyone who looked cross-eyed at the mogul.

"If Zack says go ahead, then by all means, ask him about the Playbill," she echoed. "If he says change course, you're prepared to do that?"

"I always listen to you," he said, smiling.

"Yeah, right."

Bo wrapped his arms around her and pressed his lips against hers. The possibility of getting his great-great uncle a mention in the Playbill made him feel good, turning his mind to amorous thoughts. The bills she'd set on the table could wait.

CHAPTER 31

Aimee couldn't believe her luck. She'd just picked through an online jazz events website and found that Bo's idol Stef Dalton was playing a small club in Manhattan. It was a weekday, which could be a problem with work, but the odds were good that he'd jump at the chance. At 94 years young, there was no certainty that Stef would have many more performances.

She called the club, a cute-sounding place named The Minor Seventh, but they told her it was sold out. "Do you have seats for the press?" she asked.

"Are you the press?"

She hung up.

Desperation set in. This would be the perfect opportunity to get Bo in a social setting without seeming too obvious; it wasn't a *date*, it was a lucky break – a coincidence, that's all. What she really wanted was for him to notice her in a personal kind of way. If only she could land a few tickets...

Then she remembered a connection she had, a chip she'd never called in, which could probably get her what she needed.

When she wasn't serving patients their meals, long before she worked in the ER, Aimee had been a singer-actress in community theater. The last time she acted was two years earlier as the lead in a modern-day spin on "Guys and Dolls." The production had a short run in an off-off Broadway venue and her performance caught the attention of a well-known theater reviewer from the New York Sun. He reached out to the producer who pleaded with Aimee to take the interview. She had no designs on going into acting full-time, but she agreed. It would give the play some important coverage.

The reviewer arranged to meet her after a Saturday performance. She had changed into her street clothes and was about to step outside to meet him when she was delayed by a drunk set designer who had asked her out for a drink and was being a douche about it. Finally, she was able to free herself from his drama and walked out the back door.

The theater reviewer had waited twenty minutes and was just about to leave when he saw Aimee. "I thought you weren't coming," he said, pleased to see this gorgeous, dark-haired actress up close. "But I'm glad you're here." It was a frigid February night, and she was shivering.

"I won't keep you," he continued. "My name is Mike Machado and I review plays for the Sun. I just wanted to say I loved your performance."

"I thought you wanted to interview me?" she asked.

"They don't want me to write about Off-Off plays, sorry. But personally speaking, you can really sing jazz, incredibly so. As well as anyone else I've seen in the biz." Why was he really here? It was damn cold.

"Seriously, it's not a come-on," he said. "I have connections all over. You ever want to explore singing full-time and maybe get auditions higher up on the food chain, feel free to drop my name or give me a call." He slid his business card into her hand.

"Thank you, that's very generous," she said.

Aimee never called him. While she loved theater, she had just started at the hospital and wanted to stay where there were benefits and a pension. It also looked like Matt Singelli was about to pop the question and she'd have to deal with that too.

She wasn't thinking of Matt now, though. She was thinking about the business card that was still tucked away in her wallet. Maybe with this guy's connections she could get her hands on tickets to see Stef Dalton.

CHAPTER 32

On her lunch break, Aimee walked to one of the hospital's small family-friendly lounges. She took out the business card and dialed her long-ago admirer.

"Hi, talk." It was a strange way to answer the phone.

"Hello Mr. Machado, this is Aimee Patel, we met outside my community theater for 'Guys and Dolls' two years ago."

Mike Machado knew exactly who she was. All that stuff about not coming on to her was baloney. He'd hook up with her in a New York minute.

"Hi Aimee, I remember you, of course. And call me Mike."

"Thanks, Mike. Well, the reason for my call is unfortunately not to grow a new career. But I do have a favor to ask, if it is at all possible..." Aimee's voice trailed off. If he was like every other man she knew, he was hot for her and not beyond pulling some strings to do her a favor.

"I'm intrigued. And I'm not often intrigued." He laughed. "Tell me what you need. If I can do it, I will."

Aimee exaggerated her affinity for jazz and told him she was trying to get tickets to see Stef Dalton but they were sold out. "I don't know if this is in your realm of power" – he'd like that word, she thought – "but if there is any way at all to score a few tickets to his show, it would really help me out."

"Let me see what I can do," he said. "I hope you're still singing, Aimee. It's one of your best qualities."

Men were so transparent.

Aimee was in luck, in a big way.

Mike Machado came through with six tickets. Not wanting to be rude, she accepted them all, thinking she'd give the others away at the door.

Then she had a thought. She'd quietly canvass her friends from the other departments and see if any of them were jazz fans. If she could get four other people to come along, it might seem less threatening to Bo, and if he didn't feel like it was inappropriate, he'd probably say yes.

It was just pure serendipity that the show was on a Thursday, the same night Matt taught from six to nine. He often ended class by inviting the students to a local diner to talk about the screwed-up state of contemporary politics. This would keep Matt occupied for the evening. Naturally, she'd tell him she was going to the club, but if she could say "a bunch of us from work are going out" then it wouldn't be a lie.

All the signs pointed to Bo being attracted to her: those quick glances, the sheepish smiles and the time he spent in the office alone with her talking about music. That had to count for something.

She'd not met many people like Bo. He never badmouthed his wife. He was always respectful. It was annoying. *There's a chink in that armor somewhere, it's just well-hidden.*

The plan was to let Bo bask in his musical dreamland during Dalton's first set. Then, when there was a break, she'd find a way to get him alone and make a move.

All she wanted was a few minutes alone with him to get close enough to feel his heat and look him in the eyes; to confirm that he was into her. If he didn't turn tail, that would prove he wanted her just as much. That was basically all she was hoping for; but if it went any further, she'd be open to the possibilities.

This was a delicious time in her life where she could enjoy the best of both worlds. Matt Singelli was smitten with her, and for a 54-year-old, was almost goofy about it. He was willing to wait for her to become more established at the hospital, maybe another year, before they'd get married. That gave her plenty of room and plenty of time to execute her plan and get Bo out of her system once and for all. Whether it would work that way was another story altogether.

CHAPTER 33

There was just one thing that could go wrong. Bo could say he'd love to go...but with Margret.

Aimee prayed that his wife didn't like jazz. *Okay, even if that was unlikely,* she thought, *maybe she'd just be too tired after work.*

Aimee first met Margret when Bo brought her around to say goodbye before moving on to St. Cecil's.

"That's Aimee, she's in patient registration," she heard Bo say from the hallway. They stepped into the office and Bo absentmindedly squeezed his wife's shoulder.

"This is my bride, Margret." As if Aimee didn't know. Did he have to say *bride*? That was a little much.

"Hi, how're you?" Aimee mumbled.

And now, you may leave.

"Good, thanks," she responded. "Just saying my County Memorial goodbyes before moving on to St. Cecil's."

Don't worry, I'll keep him company when you go.

Bo introduced her to the rest of the techs, half of whom were new. There was a lot of turnover in the department he was supposed to fix, but how, he had no idea. The registration and tech jobs didn't pay well and were usually just a stepping stone to other departments after they burned out from the ER. Margret said a warm hello to the familiar faces and shook hands with the new staffers. They all seemed so young, she thought. Her gaze momentarily got stuck on Aimee.

As they left the office, Bo turned back to his staff and caught Aimee's look of annoyance. Whatever she was miffed about was her problem, not his.

CHAPTER 34

What was the best way to let Bo know he was going to see Stef Dalton in person? That was Aimee's happy dilemma. If his gratitude made him feel warm and fuzzy about her, it was all the better.

She looked like the cat that ate the canary. Bo noticed.

"Got your insurances verified for the morning?" he asked, trying to steer the conversation. She had a smile plastered on her face and it was bothering him.

"Yes sir."

"Well, you don't need to be that official."

She laughed. "It's just that – what would you say if I told you I have something exciting in my pocket?"

Bo was hoping this wasn't going to be a situation, and then two other registration reps came into the office. *Thank God.*

"What's up?" he asked, loudly enough to include the others.

"Yes Aimee, what's up?" one of them mimicked. Aimee wasn't really a team player and her co-workers had no patience for her coyness.

"It just so happens," she said, unfazed, "that I have tickets to Bo's favorite musician of all time. He's into jazz, you know."

They knew; she'd already asked them if they wanted to come. Fortunately, they both said no.

"What do you mean?" Bo was trying to think ahead but didn't know where this was leading.

Aimee removed a ticket from her notebook and placed it on his desk. "Just a little music in a place called The Minor Seventh."

He couldn't believe his eyes. There was no way he'd pass up on this performance, which, at this point, could unfortunately be Stef's last one. *What did she want for it?* he wondered.

"Wow, Aimee. I don't know what to say. How much will that set me back?"

So far, so good; he hadn't asked about who else was going, even though another ticket was sticking out of her notebook.

"I called in a favor. Some guy saw a community theater play I was in and got his hot little hands on these."

By this point the other reps knew what was up. One rolled her eyes at the other, who had to leave the office before bursting out laughing. Aimee couldn't care less.

"So how about it? Wanna go?"

Before he could respond – he hadn't even checked the date – she let him off the hook. Slightly.

"I found out that John Eckley from Accounting is into jazz. He's bringing his son, who's in marching band,

and he's also an Eagle Scout. I gave two more to my friends from the cafeteria."

Bo did a quick calculation and realized that left two tickets, for him and Aimee. *Oh boy.*

"What about your fiancé?" he asked, tensing slightly.

"Teaching."

Just great.

"Let me check with Margret and see if she has anything planned for us that day. Can I let you know?"

"Sure thing."

She knew what his answer would be. He wouldn't miss it for the world.

CHAPTER 35

Bo was about to call Zack about whether he should keep the meeting with Fetterman when another bunch of solid caps came through his email. According to Bernard Fetterman's auto reply, the producer was called out of town on a project that would revive the larger-than-life Busby Berkeley movies from the 1930s. *If he has the budget for this, he is for sure wealthy,* thought Bo.

Dear Mr. Fetterman,

I see you are unable to meet for a quick coffee and that's no problem at all. I just wanted to tell you again how much I liked 'Scandals of Violet.' As crazy as it sounds, one of your songs reminds me of something my great-great uncle had written! He was enslaved on one of the major plantations and family lore has it he was a musician. It was handed down and my grandmother used to sing it to me when I was little. I'd love to share it with you one day. Anyway, thanks again for the ticket and good luck on your new movie venture.

Bo Sonski -Abbott

He hoped it sounded intriguing to the old man, but not like a veiled threat over a copyright issue. It wasn't until after he sent it that he wondered if he should have gotten a thumbs up from Zack first. No harm done, though. It was bland enough, wasn't it?

Bernie Fetterman wouldn't respond to Bo's email; at least not immediately. One day soon, though, he'd have quite a bit to say to Bo, and it wasn't pretty.

CHAPTER 36

She was cute, petite and career-minded. A trifecta that attracted him despite knowing better.

When Aimee brought him the ticket to Stef Dalton's performance, he knew his will would be severely tested.

Margret probably wouldn't want to come anyway, but she would definitely have appreciated a choice in the matter. When Bo told her how he got the ticket, a pang of heat ringed his collar. She arched her right eyebrow, then he saw it go back in place. "You should go," she said.

"You don't mind?"

"I'm serious, Bo," she said, sensing his discomfort. "If Chickiepoo makes a move on you, and don't think I didn't notice how she looked at me that time in your office, just tell her about the Glock you got me and that my aim is pretty damn good." She had a gun locked away in a closet and she went to the range a few times a year, just to stay sharp. Hopefully she was kidding about using it.

Bo planted a slow one on Margret and pulled back to look into her eyes. "Nobody would dare mess with me, you know that, baby," he purred.

"They'd better not."

CHAPTER 37

Bo typically hung out by the ambulance bay to stay in the middle of things just in case. He didn't monitor the reps' every move but he wanted them to know he was there if they needed help. The unit supervisors, the core of nerve central for the ER nurses, came to appreciate his presence. He was good at managing his staff and was a rolling-up-the-shirtsleeves kind of guy. More than once he'd ease the tension by talking with the patients' family members who were freaked out to be there.

When things were really slow, he worked on music, composing on the fly from a document on his desktop. Little song snippets could eventually add up to something, and at the end of every day he'd forward whatever he'd written to his home email.

One afternoon while he was writing a song, he realized the time had gotten away from him. It was quiet in the ER but that didn't mean things wouldn't get crazy in a second.

He saved his document and closed it, getting ready to roll his COW around to see what the reps were up to.

"You're coming to see Stef, right?" Aimee had all but ambushed him in the Trauma hallway.

"Yes ma'am. Margret is too exhausted after work. And we'll get to hang out with John and his son. Fun times!"

She smiled. He did say "we."

CHAPTER 38

The stress of an evening with Aimee around almost caused him to cancel. Was there something buried deep inside that was whimpering to get out? Even if he would never do or say anything inappropriate, he knew precisely how a night out with live jazz made him feel, and now, after all the anxiety had built up and with a beautiful employee less than a foot away, it was extremely uncomfortable yet, strangely, confusingly pleasant.

This is the last place I should be, he admonished himself. Then he saw Stef Dalton step up to the stage.

Aimee was already sitting at a large table and she waved him over. To one side were her friends from the cafeteria. John and his boy sat at the other end. The empty seat right next to Aimee was for him. It took a few seconds to gather himself. Once he looked to the stage and saw Dalton tuning his D string, he felt better. *That's really why I'm here.*

Bo glanced at Aimee and saw a cheerfulness he hadn't yet seen at work. She flashed a smile and pulled out his chair, then turned back to her friends.

A radio station, fuzzy with interference, ping-ponged around in his head. He tried to tune into something definitive but found two conflicting signals. The first said *sit down, idiot. This is your night. Take what she's offering, and don't pretend you don't know what that is.* The other said *don't ruin your life for this girl. Get up. Get out. Go home.*

I'm not doing this angel/devil thing, he thought. *I'm just here at a club listening to my idol walk all the hell over that bass and do his thing. I happen to be with a very attractive young lady, but so what! There are attractive people all around me. Mags would understand. And John Eckley is here from work, with his son, for crying out loud.*

The moment the match head strikes the flint and you smell the sulfur – right before it takes flame – that was the irresistible limbo he was in. He had to admit, it was very tantalizing. Maybe he could stay on the balance beam and nothing more would happen. Before the matchstick became fire.

The band had launched into its sixth tune, Brubeck's "Greensleeves" in three-quarters time. Eyes closed, body swaying, Dalton plucked that bass like it was the last woman he would ever hold. His lows rumbled and gave texture to the music. His high notes sang out sweetly, effortlessly, flawlessly.

The 92-year-old was working up quite a sweat. It wouldn't be much longer before he signaled to the musicians to stop for their break.

Sure enough, one last chord was held to deafening applause, then finally, released. The house lights went up for the first set's intermission.

Aimee was still standing and clapping, and Bo was right next to her doing the same. Their arms touched. He edged away. She noticed but didn't correct it. "Wow, Bo. They're really something else. What do you think?"

Bo's eyes were shining. It was ecstasy being so close to his favorite musician of all time. "Thank you, Aimee, for bringing me here. I just don't know what to say."

I can think of quite a few things, thought Aimee.

"I'm going to stretch my legs and hit the bathroom," he added. He thought he was getting some much-needed distance from her and was oblivious to her upcoming scheme, but he played right into it.

Aimee watched him go partway down the corridor and make a left into the men's room. It was only two doors away from the coat room. She followed after him. "Good time to freshen up. See you in a few."

Once inside the bathroom, she tore her bag open to find her toothbrush with a dab of paste already on it. She shoved it under the cold tap water and ran it over her teeth. Then she ducked into a stall, took out a pre-moistened washcloth she had brought from home and washed the important parts. She came out, checked herself in the mirror and nodded. "Get it, girl!"

She exited the ladies' room, having timed it just right. Bo was in the hallway looking at the black and white photos on display. They went back to the 1940s, depicting the jazz artists who had performed there; some famous, some about to be.

It was now or never.

"Bo?" she said timidly.

"Yes?" he asked. He had no idea what was about to happen.

"I saw this room over here. It must have been a coatroom to the stars. Come take a look."

Now, Bo was not a naïve guy. But he thought it would take a lot of nerve for this woman to make a pass at him, and he couldn't picture anything happening in such a public space.

He was wrong: he *was* naïve.

Aimee led the way with Bo following closely behind her. As soon as they entered the claustrophobic darkness, Aimee turned around and stepped up to him. They were inches apart.

"Bo, please. I just want one thing." And giving him no time to react, she brought her arms up around his neck while she licked her lips and leaned forward.

Bo shot backwards, escaping her kiss, but he could feel Aimee's body heat and smell the alcohol on her breath. She tried to press into him but he took a step to the side, pushing the coats out of the way. Now several feet separated them.

What the hell! He turned on his heels to head back into the club, struck speechless by the mix of anger, confusion and arousal that was trampolining inside his chest. He vowed to take control of himself. There would be no more battling forces between his conscience and his weaker nature, which he hadn't acknowledged until now.

The sensations remained as he returned to his chair, even as he watched Dalton check his strings and get ready to play. Missing even a minute of the musician's activity would be a sin. He regretted his own vulnerability and stupidity, but then again, nothing really happened. He'd not done anything wrong.

He scooted over towards John. "A refill, please," he motioned to the passing waitress. His heart was still pounding.

Aimee came back over to the table and threw down a ten. She was pissed. She had fabricated an interest in jazz to get closer to him and went through the trouble of getting tickets to the show (and would probably hear back from Machado to reciprocate the favor).

She stood behind him and dramatically zipped up her jacket. "You were the one sending out signals," she hissed. "But whatever. Enjoy your show."

Before he could say anything – before he could even decide if he wanted to respond – Aimee grabbed her handbag and strode out onto a windy Seventh Avenue to find a cab.

Bo's heart was still doing flip-flops. John shot him a sympathetic look. Things had gone too far; he had to snap back to reality. Put it in a little box and throw away the key, that's what he'd do.

A rivulet of relief was beginning to seep in, knowing she was gone and probably wasn't coming back. Her friends didn't seem to care. They were three sheets to the wind, anyway.

When he looked back up to the stage, he took a deep breath and reset himself. He was ready to concentrate on the music.

The band's next tune was "Little Boy Blue." Dalton was playing to Bo's pain.

CHAPTER 39

Bo texted Margret: *Staying for set #2, he's great!* He had calmed down enough to talk to John, whose son was clearly star-struck over Stef Dalton.

The show pumped a new passion into Bo. How amazing it was to be able to perform for an audience, and hearing a great like Dalton was unforgettable, definitely a bucket list item. He took it all in, studying the bassist's face, analyzing his posture, watching his finger placement and his right foot keeping time. Dalton was famous for his Picasso-like stoop over the formidable instrument. He was in his own world. The other musicians onstage took his lead, clearly enraptured to be playing with such an icon, and they all meshed seamlessly.

After the set was done, Dalton, who was dripping with sweat, gave a nod to Bo, whom he noticed had some issues earlier with a pretty female. Bo smiled and pulled out a chair (Aimee's chair) welcoming him to the table. What a surprise when he heard Stef say, "Love to, man," as he approached.

"God a'mighty, Mr. Dalton, what a great groove tonight!" Bo said.

The old man laughed, which exaggerated the lines in his face, etched deep as if by a jigsaw drill. Many hard years, Bo guessed.

"Thank you, my friend," said the musician, graciously bowing. "And you are?"

"Beauregard Sonski-Abbott, but please call me Bo. I'm a bass player too. Well, compared to you, a hobbyist."

"I'm sure you are no such thing. If you can play that monster, you are no hobbyist." Dalton's eyes crinkled, and he threw a glance around him. Knowing the answer, he asked Bo, "Nobody needs this chair?"

What a character. He's toying with me.

"Nope, not anymore," Bo responded, turning red. "Anyway, can I buy you a drink?" Bo asked, already gesturing over to the waitress.

"Now we're talking. Sure thing, scotch neat. Thank you." Dalton settled back into the chair. "Tell me where you play. What you play."

Bo could hardly believe his luck in scoring a sit-down with this giant of the art form. He was so grateful to the universe that Aimee had left the club...for so many reasons.

"I haven't played in a club since college."

"Oh, like last year?" Dalton chided.

"No sir," said Bo. "I'm not that young. It's been over 15 years. I own a Juzek. It's a highly decent fiddle, not quite entry-level. It was what I could afford at the time."

"No crime there. I bet you can knock some sense into that thing."

Bo smiled. "I try my best."

The band was breaking down the stage. Dalton didn't want anybody handling his bass and waved them away from it. "Well, I need to get to the head real quick and then finish packing up. It's almost beddy-bye for Stef." He stuck out his hand. "Gotta go home and plunge these arthritic digits into ice and rub some Tiger Balm on the whole body. Nice meeting you."

"Great meeting you," Bo agreed. "You saved my night."

The old man smiled and pointed to his chair. "I hear that. Nobody needs that drama, am I right?"

"You can say that again."

CHAPTER 40

It was a week since the disastrous night with Aimee. Every day since then, she refused to make eye contact with him. Bo decided he had to say something before it went on too long; to see if there was trouble ahead like a plan to ruin his career or worse, his marriage.

The office was empty and Aimee was right outside the door, standing at her COW and watching the screen. For the moment, there were no ambulances or walk-ins. It was uncharacteristically quiet in the ER.

Bo was scared to death but he had to try to reset the employee-supervisor dynamic. Finding courage from necessity, he opened the door and stepped into the hallway. "Aimee, can I please talk to you in the reception area?"

Being in confined quarters alone together would be a mistake, which was why he didn't suggest they go into the office. The reception area was much safer, out in the open, with only the two front desk staffers who were watching videos on their phones.

Reluctantly, she followed him down the hall to a corner of the huge reception area. He stopped and waited for her under a giant TV. In plain sight yet unable to be heard was best.

It was clear from the narrowing of her eyes that she was furious and hurt. There was something else too, that he couldn't know: she was worried that Bo might expose her to Matt. She needed Matt, even though she knew something was missing with him.

"Before you say anything, Bo, I want to tell you I'm sorry." Coming from Aimee, this was a switch.

"For what, exactly?" Bo asked, trying to keep his voice flat.

"For putting you on the spot. For pushing myself on you. For basically asking you out – and knowing you're married. That was my doing and a really bad idea."

God, he was so relieved. But she had more to say.

"Still. You've been making these stupid googly-eyes at me for weeks, and I'm wondering to myself what the hell does this man want?" Now Aimee was getting worked up. Bo had to talk her off the ledge and get her to calm down. If anybody heard her, things would go from bad to worse.

She wasn't entirely wrong, because he definitely felt something, at least initially, but in a "back in the day I would definitely date her" kind of way. He was no dog. He'd never cheated on Margret, though Lord knew there had been opportunities, as there surely must have been for Margret. "I'm so sorry, Aimee. I never meant for you to think of me as flirting with you. It was wrong to go to the club with you, although you can definitely pick a great show." Aimee allowed a smile. "I actually told Margret that we were going with some other people from work. She was cool with it because she knows how

I idolize Stef Dalton." He paused, then capped things off. "I'm really sorry if you've read me wrong."

Time hung in the air. Aimee moved her mouse around and watched the screen, not saying a word.

Bo tried to remember if he'd ever said anything inappropriate that made him look like he was interested. He really didn't think so. It was true that he might have been momentarily attracted to her when she started, but he didn't think it showed.

Margret was always saying he was oblivious when it came to reading people. He'd definitely have to work on that if Aimee was going to stay in his department, and if he wasn't somehow going to get fired. He needed to pay more attention to how people reacted to him, especially this one.

"If we can," he offered, "I'd like for us to go back to being two poor slobs who work together and just want to help the day go a little faster." It was asking a lot.

"Sure," she said, icily. She was angry again. "But you give me that moonstruck look again and I'm going to report you. I really don't need the insecurities of a pussified married man to complicate my life."

And though he didn't quite relate to the words she had just said, you didn't need to tell Bo something twice.

Aimee clicked on a room and without another word, pushed her COW towards the ambulance bay. The screen had lit up and suddenly four other registration reps wheeled out of the hallway, each walking quickly to a different intake room. As he assessed which room to head over to first, the receptionist called out to him, "You okay?" Bo hoped he looked like he was just reprimanding a subordinate, but he wasn't sure he pulled it off. "Just peachy," he said.

CHAPTER 41

"Mags. We have to talk." Bo hated saying the words as much as he would have hated being on the receiving end of them. He didn't want to be living a cliché either, especially when so many amazing things were starting to happen. But things needed to be said.

Margret was at the dining room table, the one they had bought at an antique store in upstate New York. The feet had tin-coated talons and the warped wood was pitted from tiny, unknown traumas. It was a charming reminder of life's bumps, bruises and durability. The possibilities always seemed so poetic to Margret. Bo liked it because the color matched his bass.

"Hmm, not liking such an ominous beginning. Tell me what's up." Margret had no context for worry in their relationship. This was something new. Synapses fired in dormant parts of her brain, recalling the only blip they'd ever had. They'd just started dating and Bo told her about a woman named Dana, whom he was trying to break up with. She was a bit of a psycho. Eventually, after threatening to make a scene at his job, she faded away. Margret trusted Bo to handle it, and he definitely passed the test.

Still, her nerves were on high alert.

"Okay, first of all, this is probably nothing," he said. "But it's been eating away at me for a little over a week."

Whatever it was, was fairly recent, she told herself. And for crying out loud, it probably wasn't *that*; they didn't have those types of issues, did they?

"Remember when I went out to hear Stef Dalton play, and what an incredible night I told you it was?" Bo was sitting across from her. The scratches in the tabletop formed the J of a saxophone that he now traced with his finger. Why had he never noticed that before?

Margret resisted the onslaught of dread, but it wasn't easy. The anticipation was hurting her stomach. *Buckle up, buttercup. Here goes.* "Tell me."

"Yeah, so that girl Aimee was there."

Let me stab her eyes out right now with a kitchen knife. And maybe Bo's too. "Yeah, Bo, you told me. And I never trusted her. She likes you." She took a stuttered breath. "Go on."

"She made a move and I backed away so fast that we both almost fell. I went right back to the table. She was so mad that when she came back into the club, she grabbed her bag and left. And that was it."

First of all, Margret didn't appreciate the pronoun *our* describing the word *table*. "Remind me again who else was with you?"

"Two women from the cafeteria and John Eckley from accounting and his son. You know, the Eagle Scout."

"Got it. Was Bo being an Eagle Scout too?" Margret's face was turning red. This was a time to anger, and she wasn't going to stop it.

"Of course I was, Mags! There was a break in the music and I got up to go to the bathroom." *Damn. I'm really going to tell her this.* "As soon as I got out, Aimee was there in the hallway, looking at some cool black and white photos of musicians. She comes right up to me and almost mashes her face into mine. I had some leeway to back up, which I did. I couldn't push her away because it would have meant touching her." He was afraid to meet her eyes. "Really, Mags, there was no reason to have said anything to you before because nothing happened. But it's just been gnawing at me."

And why did he tell her – was it to clear his head or because he couldn't shake it and she could read him like a book? He just wanted to move on from it.

Margret envisioned the totality of time they'd spent together. Bo was one of the good guys, and she knew in her bones this was a nothing-burger. So why did she find herself rising out of her chair?

"Tell me all of it now or else I'm walking out." She wanted to be one hundred percent sure that he was coming clean and there was nothing more to it.

"Mags. That's all of it. She was majorly pissed off and has been taking every opportunity to give me the stink eye at work. Today there was a Code Orange and she wanted to stay behind and 'talk'. Needless to say, I didn't. But I can't afford these types of situations at work, and I don't want to lose my job over it."

"Over...?"

"Her making any allegations. Which she hasn't yet, but I feel it coming. Boy, do I feel it coming."

Margret considered the situation and sat back down. "I think you need to preemptively talk to HR and just let the chips fall. Get it out there on your personnel record. If the worst happens, you'll just have to find a new job. We'll get through it."

Bo loved Margret for many different reasons, some of which seemed inconsequential, mundane. The way she paid their bills on time, always. The way she heated his coffee cup in the microwave before the first pour of the morning. The way she left his tangled mass of papers untouched in the music room. And now, the way she believed in him. It was everything.

CHAPTER 42

"So basically, you had an emotional affair with that girl. With Aimee."

"Yes, that's her name, but no to the affair. Of any kind." Bo was not enjoying the direction this conversation was taking.

Pip Jones could always read Bo. The last time they talked was over a month ago and they'd been way overdue to nurse a few beers. He was living in Boston but came down to New York to guest conduct at the Mannes School of Music and naturally, Bo was the first person he reached out to.

"You don't think I know what it's like?" Pip asked. "Just the thought of her puts a little pep in the ol' step. Look, I get it. Some of the college students are blindingly gorgeous. But still, it's hands-off. And I'm single."

"Yeah, the younger ones keep getting prettier. But it's not what I wanted to really talk to you about."

"Got ya. Tell me more about Stef Dalton." Pip took a swallow and burped.

"There were other people there that night." Bo couldn't let it go yet. "I made sure of that. And nothing happened. It almost did, but your boy did the right thing."

"Yes, you did," said Pip. "You made me proud. I adore Mags and I'm glad you zigged when this chick wanted you to zag. Can you tell me why we're having this conversation, then?"

Bo laughed. "Good question. I guess I just needed to get it out. The whole thing threw me. I'm too old for this stuff."

"You'll get out the other side of this," said Pip. "Sounds like you already are." He sat and cocked his head, eyebrows raised. "Dalton...?"

"Yes! He was beyond amazing. Even with all the crap that went on with me. He saw her get up and leave – that's the last I'll say about it, I promise! Anyway, after the second set he sat down and we talked a bit."

"No kidding? That's awesome. How was the music?"

Pip was onto beer number two. Bo held up his hand and shook his head when the waitress asked if he wanted another.

"It was off the charts. Lots of my favorites, he really was crankin'. Everything from *How High the Moon* to *Green Dolphin Street* to *You Go to My Head* and then three Fats Waller numbers that got the place jumping."

"Sounds brilliant. I sure do miss playing."

"Have you tried?" Bo asked.

"I haven't picked up the sax in ages, except when I'm teaching, and only to demonstrate embouchure or something. It's interesting to track how the emphysema affects it."

"And?"

"If I do the exercises my doctor gave me and meditate before playing, I can blow almost like I used to."

"Fantastic!"

Pip's second beer had become room temperature. He threw it back anyway. "And you? Messing around with old Chauncey lately?"

"Yeah, well that's what I want to talk to you about. After I went to the play, when I found out about my great-great uncle and all the stuff I told you about, I started composing again."

Pip perked up. "Ahhh. Am I involved somehow?"

"You know it. I started the first song, but I want to do more." The idea clearly wasn't fully baked. Bo was making it up as he went. "I want to do a CD. My man's music needs to be heard. The idea of how his song was stolen needs to be heard." He was afraid to ask Pip anything more.

"Dude. You know I'm in."

Step one, get buy-in from your best friend: check.

CHAPTER 43

Zack was almost positive that Bo had no case when it came to calling Fetterman's alleged use of Lymus's song a case of stolen intellectual property. There was a secondary concern, and that was to ascertain the provenance of the music regardless of whether anything could legally be done about it.

Zack's wife had a cousin, Susan Wright, who was married to a rabid Civil War savant. He made a career as an expert witness to authenticate period artifacts and enjoyed an elevated status as an executive at one of the big auction houses. For fun, he appeared on "Antiques Roadshow" where he'd spout pontifications over battlefield paintings and Bakelite brooches. Slightly arrogant (and an unfaithful husband, as family buzz had it), Jamie Wright nevertheless knew his stuff down to the fine details.

"Zack, my man of the hour. How art thou?" Jamie had always talked to family members like a moron.

Zack provided a very quick catchup of life as a happily married lawyer, then explained about Bo seeing *Scandals of Violet*, his visit to the Smithsonian and the possibly misappropriated sheet music. He could tell Jamie was flattered to have been consulted.

"Send me your friend's photos of the documents. Let me take a gander."

A week later, Jamie called back. "From what I can see, your friend Bo probably has nothing to fight for. Yet--"

"Yet what?"

"Does Bo have anything with his ancestors' signatures, photos that were signed on the back, or letters? To tie the handwriting to his relative?"

"I didn't ask him that, specifically, but I will."

Jamie was silent. Was that how he finished his conversations?

"Let's just say there's nothing else to compare it to, does that make it a dead case?" Zack asked.

Jamie cleared his throat. "I'm afraid so. In that case, he can always visit it again in the museum in DC. Sorry to say, Zack."

"Well, okay. Thanks for your time, bud, and our best to Susan," he said, wincing as he said Jamie's wife's name. Maybe Jamie had changed for the better, he told himself.

Yeah. Maybe pigs would fly and a song written by a slave would be returned to its rightful heirs.

CHAPTER 44

The last Code Orange hadn't gone smoothly, and Bo needed to hold a meeting. Eight registration reps crowded into the office. It had to be quick. The ER never sleeps.

"I want to commend you all on picking off the dozen or so patient rooms and getting the job done at Monday's Code Orange. It was a terrible accident, dang that Belt Parkway! But thank God no fatalities, and all the cases got dispatched very quickly. Bravo!" Bo beamed and waited for his staff to breathe a sigh of relief. But they were squirmy. And he tried not to look, but not to *not* look, at Aimee. Why was this still weird?

"The thing is, there was one little glitch. It's in our best interest to stay glitchless."

The staff respected Bo. He was probably the least annoying department manager in the organization's dense quagmire of crisscrossing, mind-numbing, top-heavy administration.

And here comes the part where we messed up, he imagined them all thinking.

"Just please" – here it is – "watch those typos in the patient names. The blood bank upstairs has to hustle for these patients and they've got to have accurate labels in hand."

Bo paused, making sure he hadn't lost them. They were a hard-working group and very responsive, but loyalty is a fragile animal.

"There were two typos, and one was actually due to a driver's license having the wrong spelling. I know we can't be held accountable for that." He smiled briefly, trying to lighten it up. "Now, the other one – and don't go perseverating on who did what, I just want to cite it as an example – the other one was our brains trying to correct, frankly, a name spelling that's pretty uncommon." The problem was, it was Aimee's patient, who, in her haste, took "Jeffery" and typed it in as the more standard "Jeffrey."

"If you have the least bit of doubt, please, just ask one of your co-workers or even a floor nurse to confirm a spelling based on a driver's license, especially if you haven't received it in-hand. I know that seconds count, but this is one second we can afford. Any questions?"

The only question that seven of them had was the unspoken *"OK, so can we go now?"* For one of them in particular, the only other question was, "Tell me why I still care about anything you say?"

CHAPTER 45

Aimee picked apart the night at the club the way you obsess over a scab. Although Matt had become as attentive as ever (was it his increased questioning about setting a date? Was he hearing her biological clock about to go off?) she couldn't put to rest that she was rebuffed. Bo had definitely been flirting. Who the hell was he to suddenly become Mister Innocent?

She wasn't used to rejection. It occurred to her that maybe she was losing her touch, and the thought turned into the more serious fears over losing her attractiveness, becoming unlovable and a spiral of negative thinking that she didn't want to entertain. What if I'm unattractive to everybody except Matt? And the most terrifying of all: what if I fall out of love with Matt, then what?

The flame of attraction to Bo wasn't being extinguished anytime soon. Aimee could sense he was trying very hard to normalize their relationship at work. He made a special point of talking directly to her in a staff meeting; in a friendly way, but with a hidden meaning that she took as "We're cool now, right?"

No, Aimee was not cool. In fact, she was approaching angry. He at least owed her a discussion over it. Maybe even an apology.

Her chance came sooner than she would've imagined. A staff meeting was called, then cancelled, when one of the other registration reps had an emergency at home and needed to leave work. The rest of the reps were standing around in the office, watching the ER activity on their COWS. Suddenly the screens lit up like Christmas as a five-car accident involving a tractor trailer filled the ER with ambulance personnel and cops and victims on stretchers. Aimee counted quickly: three rooms switched to red, and instantly, three registration reps flew out of the office. *They need me out there,* she thought. *Just a minute or two alone with Bo and his guilty face should do it, then I'll run over to help them.*

"Bo."

He was watching the board and grabbed his COW. "Gotta run, Aimee. Come on out so we can help everybody get the reggies done and get some labels printed for the bloodwork they're pulling."

"Bo please, it'll take a second," she insisted.

This was insubordination. Bo couldn't risk any delays and knew they had to get the patients processed ASAP. "We don't have a second, Aimee. Meet me out there."

It was unthinkable that she wanted to revisit that night, especially now when there were urgent matters to take care of. They'd already discussed things; in fact, she'd apologized (and then warned him to stop staring at her). Bo thought things were back to being okay. Whatever complaints Aimee wanted to air out were on her. No more airing. Bo was just going to do his job and move forward, and push her out of his mind.

CHAPTER 46

Getting the thumbs up from Pip was a huge win but not without its concerns. His band-directing and student lessons kept him in the swim of the local music scene in Boston, but he'd not played in an ensemble since their college days. Lack of opportunity makes a player go stale, reaching for familiar jazz clichés without taking any risks.

Bo had a hunch that the new project would inject some excitement into Pip's music life. With the new techniques he learned and by continuing to take care of his health, there was no doubt that he could hit the heights of his playing again.

There were two other phone calls that still needed to be made: Joey Fritz and Tim McKnight. Bo hoped that his powers of persuasion were still sharp enough to convince them to sign on.

Margret watched him sitting and just staring at his phone. "What's up, why the long face?"

"So much has changed about recording since we last played together and I have to get up to speed fast. Also, I really don't have time to break in two new musicians. I have no idea what Joey and Tim are up to."

Margret remembered them with a warmth. Joey Fritz, the drummer, was a little out there, slightly in her face, but very animated, very funny, and from what she could tell, a solid musician. Tim was amazingly talented, and if she remembered correctly, she'd seen him play piano backwards just like Little Richard.

"The better the technology has become, the more there is to manage," he continued. "Learning Soundcloud and Apple and every other platform out there. It's a lot." That was just the tip of the iceberg. "Composing, rehearsals, production, marketing, performances…"

"I'm sure you'll learn it all pretty fast. The guys should be able to pitch in too," Margret said. "And just think of it this way, it all started because of Lymus. That's the best reason for this CD to be made."

Even with phones and texting and Skype, there was nothing like jamming in person. They might not have that luxury, especially if they had busy lives and didn't live near each other.

A raw energy started to seep into his bones. Not everybody realized their dreams to create their passion project, taking something from the past and breathing new life into it.

"I definitely have my work cut out for me," said Bo. "First thing is, I'm hoping Fritz is stateside. Pip said he's been out of the country. He can still send us his tracks but it's so much better to produce together, in person." He nuzzled her neck. She had just slid off a ponytail holder and the smooth dark hair that fell past her shoulders smelled fruity. "Tomorrow, I contact Fritz. Today, cuddling."

But Bo was too distracted and Margret could tell.

He was already envisioning the CD cover. A grainy black and white photo of four scruffy gents with dabs of yellow and purple; their instruments in silhouette behind them. He'd need liner notes. Odessa, Margret's blogger friend who wrote about the classical music scene, had won several journalism awards and was beginning to make a name for herself. If she knew anything about jazz or even liked it, maybe she could write them.

Bo always jumped several paces ahead, but that's what defined his drive. Eye on the prize. Then he realized the prize was not the CD itself, but the amazing opportunity to make music with other people who *got it*. And more than that, presenting Lymus Abbott to the world.

CHAPTER 47

There was no telling if the old number Bo had for Joey Fritz was still working, nor did he know if his friend was even in the US. According to Pip, Joey had moved to Costa Rica five years earlier with his girlfriend Lesslie, who was a VP at the ASPCA headquarters. She decided to chuck the corporate gig to personally rescue the famed abandoned dogs that roamed throughout the Central American country and dragged Joey with her.

No surprise, Joey's number was disconnected, but Bo had his last email address.

Hey Joey, thinking of getting us back together for one last romp. Making a CD because of some huge family history I just found out about. I'll leave you in suspense until you write me back. Missing you, man, so let me know! –Bo

In four minutes, Bo's phone buzzed with a new email.

Bo, long time! CD would be awesome! I got back from CR three weeks ago. I have a lot of dogs now LOL but no Lesslie. Don't worry, it was mutual. I'm in northern Jersey, near the parents. They help with the dogs. My number's in the sig line, call me. Peace out! -- J

CHAPTER 48

As he first imagined it, the CD would be made up of all instrumental tracks. Listeners could write their own stories around the music, like a museum painting without a title card explaining why the artist painted it. This would lend a simple, sparse feel to the music that didn't crowd people with clutter.

He thought of his favorite artist, Edward Hopper, an artist who could capture the slant of early morning light on New York City brownstones in a way that evoked a width of loneliness despite its peopled buildings. Hopper had been quoted as saying, "All I ever wanted to do was paint light on the side of a house." All Bo ever wanted to do was write music that would move people. Fingers crossed and God willing, he would achieve this with the perfect balance of bass, piano, sax and drums.

CHAPTER 49

With the first song "Lines for Lymus" almost completed, Bo pulled up his window to get a better view of a corner of Prospect Park. The cars lining the four lanes of Flatbush Avenue were locked in a standstill and their horns made strange music. *I can work with that.*

Enter the Devil's Tritone.

The Devil's Tritone was actually a musical interval – a sound, not a song itself. Condemned in early Christian music, it radiated an ominous feeling and the church insisted that it inspired evil. Taking the interval of the fourth (as in *Here Comes the Bride*) and raising it a mere halftone creates a sense of unease, darkness and fear that gets flushed away when it's resolved a half note up.

Bo would meet no such expectation until the very end of the song. He wrote four separate melodic sections that emphasized the forbidden interval. When it was all put together, the song had a strange swing feel. It was also a fantastic showcase for the musicians, allowing each one a solo for 15 measures (as opposed to the traditional Western 12-bar solo; 15 would augment the sensation of discomfort). The soloists would have free reign, Bo's only request being that each musician incorporated both major and minor keys. It would be called "The Devil You Know."

He had several other songs in mind. He'd have to get cracking to write and arrange them. One of them was a "tone poem" made up of lush and nuanced chords inspired by the 20th century classical master Debussy who was often studied and revered by jazz musicians. Successfully coming out with such an abstract yet delicate piece was the holy grail of contemporary jazz composition, and if Bo could pull it off, it would make the CD very respectable. This song would be dedicated to Margret. It was a slow, sultry waltz that was heavy on the brushes. Joey would know the feel Bo was going for: contemplative, chill, the way a person feels when they're sipping a glass of full-bodied Merlot with the lights on low and a brown sugar-scented candle for atmosphere.

Bo summoned his feelings of animal attraction when they met and the overwhelming rightness of being together. The burn of lust and engulfing delight of making love. The unbreakable bond of friendship and admiration. This was what he hoped to capture.

He called it "My Merlot Girl."

He already had the bare bones of another song; scraps, really, written during a subway ride into Manhattan. It centered on the walking bass line he always loved. It would be on the funky side and, just for fun, would have a fat, wailin' sax solo; whatever Pip could handle of that. He thought about calling it

"Attitude/Gratitude." The song was barely a seedling and needed a lot of love to be developed further.

Something was missing from the song lineup. Bo couldn't figure out what it was, then it struck him: levity. The album needed some lightness, a space to pull out of the netting of its deeply emotional soul.

Even Edward Hopper came up for air. For all the solemnity and loneliness in his paintings (even his well-lit nudes were humorless), there was one stand-out, one little island of hope where people smiled and relaxed. It was a short period when the painter studied families enjoying nature in Cape Cod, and the highlight piece, the outlier in terms of his career, was a young boy fishing off a pier who wore the unmistakable look of joy as he caught his first big one. It had all the characteristic shadowing and endless expanse of New England sky Hopper was known for. With this painting Hopper was able to, just temporarily, re-craft his own leaden despair. The CD needed the same sense of respite from its heavy theme. A little sweet snack for the listener.

He called it "Popcorn." By keeping the song in the upper and middle registers, it provided a chance for the musicians to trade solos at a comfortable tempo without bogging down the sound. The key of F major allowed Pip to bend into his favorite blue notes and bounce up to the top limits of his alto, while Tim would dabble in a stride piano vibe that was sure to spread joy around like peanut butter. Joey would kick the percussion into high gear with fast rolls and no echo to hold things back.

"Hon. Do you think six songs are enough?" Even though Margret wasn't a musician, she was a consumer of music.

"When it's done, it's done. If six feels right, bless it and move on. What about issuing it on vinyl?"

This was something he hadn't considered. Certainly, an expense he hadn't anticipated. But she had a point.

"There are audiophiles out there salivating to play some beautiful jazz on their shiny new turntables," she continued. "Don't disappoint them."

"No ma'am," he said, saluting her.

The CD was almost all planned out. It was turning out to be a substantial endeavor that would be interwoven with threads contributed by the other band members – once they were all on board, as he remembered to hustle to get Tim McKnight. There was so much work ahead of him, but if he wanted to be true to his vision, there was no way around that other than powering through it.

Bo was exhausted. He'd written the roadmap for the CD and was starting to get the pieces in place.

The last obstacle was the final song. It would be based on Gramma's song about the mother bird. He hadn't figured out where the tune would meander after showcasing Lymus's melody, just that it had to elicit a lot of emotion. This was the reason for the CD and it had to loom large.

Bo would be shocked to find out who his future collaborator was going to be. Everything was about to click into place.

CHAPTER 50

As he committed notes to paper, Bo realized how blessed he was to have friends who wanted to make music together. They were true professionals. Pip's playing (even when it suffered from his compromised lung capacity) was incredibly raw and intuitive, and when he soloed, he conjured up some very beautiful melodies that were not typical for tenor sax. Pip told Bo about a new ligature for his mouthpiece, which was a simple ring made of ebony wood that did away with the usual fussy hardware. He couldn't wait to use it in the recording studio.

Joey was every leader's dream: a beast on drums whose coiled-up energy inevitably exploded into a frenzied release that audiences craved. He had the skills to decimate any polyrhythmic challenge that came his way, but also the ability to prove himself sensitive and nuanced. After Bo reached out to him, he was in with a vengeance.

Onto Tim McKnight. This was to be no small feat; he traveled extensively for his job.

Tim would bring a wealth of experience to the table. His background was in classical music with a specialty in the Baroque period from which he learned to play with breathtaking dexterity. He could slay a counterpoint like nobody's business. The only one of the group to have performed at a jazz festival (Port St. Lucie), Tim was on his way up in the world. While playing at a restaurant near his home in the Florida panhandle, he'd met a rep from Decca Records and signed a one-year contract, eventually joining the company to help find new talent. Bo had serious doubts whether Tim would be available to do the CD due to his globe-hopping. What an asset, though; he could shine like the sun and had a creative side Bo couldn't come close to. Why they lost touch, Bo had no idea.

All he had was Tim's work email. He shot off a message on his laptop with his fingers and arms crossed for luck.

Hey Tim!

It's been a while and I'm just trying to catch up. So how are you?

I was thinking about our gigging days and you've obviously kept up with your music if you're getting this email with the Decca address (at least I hope you are). You'll never believe where I'm at with music in my life.

Dream scenario would be to have you onboard for a new project I'm working on. If not, no worries. Let's catch up, I'll tell you about it!

Bo

Tim was a newlywed who tried to stay off his work email on weekends, but he wasn't always successful.

BO!

I'm so happy to hear from you, you have no idea! Long story, but yes, Decca is going great. I got married recently! I know, hard to believe LOL. You might remember him from college, he was a year ahead of us, Kyle Wight. He's a dancer and has been in a ballet troupe in Jacksonville since he graduated. I actually played for a few of their performances.

You need to tell me more about your project, but sight unseen, I'm in, baby!
TM

Bo was so grateful to have all his guys for the CD. It meant everything to him. Now he could finally dig in to write the rest of the songs and set a timeline.

The insomnia that plagued him at precisely 2 a.m. every morning wouldn't be wasted. There was a lot to do.

CHAPTER 51

Margret sat cross-legged on their only plush recliner, a view over their sunny tree-lined street on a lazy Sunday. She was gnawing on a celery stalk, not that she needed it. She was what they called "lithe."

"You know what would be amazing?" she asked.

He wrinkled his nose at the celery. Not his favorite food. "What's that?"

"What if you wrote a piece featuring two basses...you know, for you and Stef Dalton?"

"That would be a fantasy project. Not a bad idea as an exercise to stretch my writing."

"That's not exactly what I meant," Margret said. She looked at him and held his glance. "I mean, for you and him to play."

Bo stopped chewing on a carrot stick. "What, like ask him to be on the CD?"

Margret made synaptic connections that would never occur to him.

"I do. You saw him that night. You talked. You're fresh in his mind."

Bo exhaled with a whistle. "I'd have to find his press agent and go through channels. But imagine if? Wow!" His excitement quickly soured as he thought of all the potential obstacles. Dalton was one of the elder statesmen of jazz and was probably in hot demand. Right now, he could be touring Norway or in the middle of recording in LA or performing at Lincoln Center... anything was possible.

Margret found three strings sticking out the top of the celery. She pulled them with her teeth, then chewed them. Bo shuddered.

"It's probably easier than you think," Margret said. "My friend Odessa, the one who writes the classical music blog, says she gets access to Philharmonic musicians and conductors without an issue, even the really famous ones who've been featured in The New York Times." Bo cocked his head.

"All I'm saying is, just ask Dalton if he wants to work with you, just one song. He might say yes. I'm sure he'll remember you."

He would remember Bo, and Bo's pretty colleague, that's for sure. *Shake it off, bro. Nothing happened.*

"I can see it," Bo said, grateful for the encouragement. "I mean, the guy seemed to take a liking to me. I have no idea what his workload might be with gigs, but based on his steamin' set that night he sure doesn't seem to be running out of energy."

One of the best things about being married to Margret was a mixture of hard-nosed practicality juxtaposed with the belief that almost anything was possible. There was no reason Bo couldn't take a stab at this. If Dalton were unable for whatever reason, even writing a song featuring two basses and dedicating it to the master would be unique. He could mail the finished project to Dalton and maybe the old guy would talk it up. Couldn't hurt for PR.

Imagining if he said yes to being on the CD was out of proportion with reality. *Wouldn't that be a life-changer, though?*

CHAPTER 52

Lymus's original inspiration for the music he penned in cryptic notation was the hope that, one day, he and his family would be granted freedom. Whether this could happen in his lifetime, he didn't know. He prayed for it several times a day. While he'd tried to stay positive, it wasn't always possible.

On a handful of extremely rare occasions, the master's wife allowed Lymus a few stolen minutes to tinker on the piano. Sometimes these opportunities came in the silent hours of the night, when she'd caution him to lay a towel on the strings underneath the piano lid. No matter how sleepy he was, he jumped from his cot, grabbed a pencil and a swatch of jute fabric he'd hidden away and stepped lightly to the music room.

He lowered himself onto the highly sheened mahogany bench and sat at the very edge of his haunches, literally, for a slave, a death-defying position. Yet he was insanely excited to feel the full horizon of the piano keys before him. Such a singular set of circumstances, allowing him to be seated where the wife and daughter had taken lessons and played hymns, could lead to his demise; but the sense of amazement was dizzying and he was unable to break away.

He pressed each key with an angel's delicate touch, in awe of the music that resulted in the tones which radiated from the house when Master Jerrett Middleton's daughter, Callista, had played only hours before. He allowed his fingers to experience their own wanderlust north and south on the keys, correctly guessing that if he spaced them out further the resulting harmonies would produce a richness he'd only dreamed about.

Fearful of overstaying his invitation, Lymus caressed the keys only for the time that lived between quarter-hour chimes on the grandfather clock. It was enough time, though, to develop his own method of musical notation, as he didn't know how to read music conventionally. He thought he must be stupid for not being able to make sense of the confusing explosion of ink on the large sheaves scattered on top of the piano, and would never live to hear that he was a genius in his own right. He only knew to mark each note (with a line, dot or cross) in a different position on the fabric scraps he found littered about the plantation. Nobody, he thought, will ever be able to make sense of this.

There was danger in the stillness of the night where his music became so exposed, and there was danger in trusting Master Middleton's wife who could sell him out at the drop of a hat if her husband became ferocious for any number of reasons, which was always likely; one of the hallmarks of alcohol abuse. There was a risk in holding the young Callista in his heart, but more risk in falling in love with the music, because it reeked of being a free man.

Each time he was told he could use the piano, he allowed himself to think about his dear Callista, her beauty, her innocence and the most unsuitable object of his affection. No matter what, no matter how few moments were doled out to him at the piano, he would heed the calling to write a song for her. A song!

One day, in an impossible future, maybe he could play it for her.

CHAPTER 53

Callista had obviously left this for him – a wooden box just outside his living quarters – engraved as it was with the simple "2L" (*To Lymus*) on the back. This was sufficient to get him beaten, even killed. He considered scratching off the dedication.

The box was only about four inches long, four wide and two tall, but quite heavy, the detritus of a tree trunk that had fallen on the ground. A series of images was carved into the wood, and then a separate piece, like a mandala, was set on top of the lid. It depicted a bird in flight, high above the trees, with the sun a semi-circle at the top right edge, rays streaming down through the trees. It was the most beautiful thing Lymus had ever seen and his breath caught in his lungs just looking at it.

Surely there was affection in the gesture, he thought. A twinkle of excitement fluttered in his chest. A key was affixed to the back of it (*A music box!* he almost called out) but he was terrified to turn it just yet; it might be too loud. He waited until he was sure of his privacy.

A break came in his duties. It was after dinnertime and the women were finishing clean-up. Lymus had secreted the box under a pile of leaves far enough from the house to be discovered. He ran into the woods, risking injury with the many hollows in the ground that might cause him to break his ankle. He was limber and light and most of all, quiet.

Lymus looked around. Nobody was nearby and he couldn't hear the kitchen staff's chatter anymore. Removing his shirt to muffle the sound of twisting the key, he stood, gleaming with sweat, heart pounding through every vessel in his body. He squatted to decrease his visibility, knowing this small indiscretion could cost him his life. His mother would be devastated if he were found. And what of his younger sister and brother? But he had to know what music lived coiled inside of it.

As he slowly turned the key, wincing at each audible click, he wondered what it might play; what dulcet notes would pour out. He kept his shirt over the box hoping to stifle any sound it might emit. The tension had him light-headed; he squeezed his eyes shut to will away the dizziness. What music was waiting to reveal itself to him? Perhaps it would be a brazen march, or a sweet etude or a chorus of "The Battle Hymn." Lymus had heard of such music boxes but had never *heard* one. Several more clicks were all he could stand. Holding the key in check, he gently placed the box in the grass, fragrant with magnolia petals, and, holding his breath, released the key. *This could be the last earthly sound I ever hear.*

The music played. It was (but he could not know this) Beethoven's "Für Elise." At once, Lymus felt the sweeping pulse of the song. It was dark like a rain storm packaged in a waltz, the most stunning music ever to reach his ears. Tears tumbled down his cheeks. He felt foolish for all of it. For having to hide his love, for having to hide himself and this beautiful music. If he ever got out of here, he vowed, he would play this song until the day of his natural death. And even if he would never have her by his side, there was an inscription of a mere two characters which meant everything to him.

CHAPTER 54

The *quattro fabuloso* were on Zoom to put together a strategy for the CD. Their careers and busy lives left precious little time or resources to roll out their upcoming album. The launch event would be the blowout they'd never forget, but unless it made them a commercial success it had to be a one-and-done project.

Bo told them about the idea Margret had to invite Dalton for a walk-on. They agreed that getting him would be incredible.

Pip asked if anybody knew the costs of making a CD and pressing vinyl. "I can price those things out," said Joey. "In any case, we also need a graphic artist and/or a photographer. Any ideas? We need a pro shot or some hip artwork with our photos for the front and back covers."

The myriad details – recording and uploading, sound production, media and marketing, artwork, liner notes – were not exhausting but energizing. It was biting off a lot but, split four ways, it was manageable. With all his guys together, this was a golden chance at something he'd always wanted to do, creating original music that would move people.

"One more thing," continued Bo. "As far as a vocalist, I think we should be open to it. What does everybody think? We can have traditional lyrics or spoken word or a combination."

"I thought you wanted it to be all instrumental?" Tim asked.

"I did, originally. But now I'm thinking for texture. Otherwise, we might be alienating people who like vocals."

They loved the idea, but of course, somebody had to find a singer.

There was about to be one in the pipeline that would make the CD an unstoppable force.

CHAPTER 55

Pip had lists for every little thing, from the brand names of all the reeds he'd ever bought to the sax mouthpieces he'd used, favorite artists (dead and living) and his favorite songs (which numbered over 2,000) and most important his favorite sax solos (there were pages and pages of them in his spiral notebook). Now Bo had a list too, with all the moving parts of this huge project. He shared it with the others and was amazed to find he'd missed quite a few details. Of greatest importance on the massive spreadsheet was securing the venue and a release date, then working backwards to sketch out the arc of producing the CD...and a tiny detail that involved a personal meeting with Stef Dalton to explore whether the bassist had any interest in joining the project.

Though it was slightly uncomfortable to revisit the scene of the almost-catastrophe, Bo decided to face his anxiety and head over to the jazz club straight from work. He changed into a Dizzy Gillespie T-shirt that had been a gift from Margret when they started dating, so by now, it was the softest shirt he owned. It was a collage of drawings of Dizzy and included the iconic image of his cheeks swollen to inhuman proportions.

"Excuse me, but can I speak to the owner, please?" Bo's eyes darted past the bar into the kitchen, hoping to catch a glimpse of the owner or his wife, who ran the front, but was known to catch her cigarette break near the industrial refrigerator against the back wall.

"One minute, sir," the barkeep said, giving a slight smile. "You looking to sign a gig here or something?" he asked, as he started to make his way to the kitchen.

"No, not yet," Bo smiled back. "Someday, maybe soon. Just have a question for him."

The owner was a ham-handed man who used to pound the piano. He started the club when his arthritis became so bad that he couldn't play anymore. "What's up, my man? I'm Jesse. What can I do for you?" He extended his hand to Bo, who took it and nodded.

"Hey, so, a few weeks back," Bo's voice was starting to strain with excitement, "I was enjoying the amazing sounds of Mr. Stef Dalton. Wow, what a night!"

Jess chuckled. "Yeah, that guy was cookin'. I'm glad you liked the show. Come to think of it, I remember seeing you."

"Cool. So I was wondering. I play bass, but it's not my day job, you know the tale. Anyway, I'm about to make my first CD, and myself and the other three musicians are wondering if Dalton would possibly want to collaborate with us." Bo took a deep breath, then quickly added that he had actually gotten a chance to talk with Dalton between sets that evening and that Dalton seemed amiable. Whether it was enough for him to agree to work on a project with Bo, well, that remained to be seen.

Jesse chuckled again, then waved the air in front of him. "I wish Kimmy would quit smoking," he said, thumbing back to the kitchen where his wife stuck her tongue out at him. "She's got thyroid cancer but quitting has been an absolute bear for her. We're all works in progress."

Bo looked down and felt embarrassed asking for a favor. "For sure, we are."

"I think she'll beat it since it's early, thank God. So anyway, that's great news, man, a CD! Congrats. I'm not sure about passing along his cell number, but what if I tell him you were asking about him and wanted to meet?"

Bo couldn't believe what Jesse just said. "Yeah, absolutely, that would be fantastic! I'll write down my info. Please remind him we talked that night, and I was sitting with some people from work, including a young lady he complimented. Not my wife, just a co-worker, but I know he'll remember her."

Jesse was beginning to warm up to Bo and decided to give him an insider's tip. "If you really want to connect with him, he's been coming in on Sundays to have some eggs over easy around 8 in the morning. Just because he likes my ambience." He laughed. "So he says."

Bo knew that nothing would be more pressing on Sunday than to slip in to say hello to his all-time idol, hand over a business card and make his exit. He couldn't wait for the weekend. "I have one more thing to ask of you," he said to Jesse. "It's a biggie."

"Lay it on me."

"What would it take for us to have the release party here? I'll bring my bass and play for you so you can hear what I do, and I can send you some songs from the other guys."

This could bring lots of warm bodies in the door, and despite what Bo might have thought about the club being packed all the time, shows were slow and far between. Jesse had hellacious medical bills from Kim's chemo.

"Abso-fricken-lutely. Let me look at our schedule. I have to work around my wife's appointments. She just got sick."

"I'm so sorry, Jesse. My mom battled it and it's not easy. We think it's in remission."

"Glad to hear that. And thank Jesus, we got it early. Kim might be okay with a partial thyroidectomy, and heavy meds are taking on the work of the poor little organ. The good news is, they think they can curtail it spreading anywhere else."

"I'm happy to hear that, man." Bo took a beat. "Ohhh...I know what to do."

"What?" asked Jesse.

"Let's make it a fundraiser to help with your medical bills. I can't think of a better reason for you and me to come together now than that."

Jesse's palms were on his face, pressing tears away from his eyes. "Thanks man. Yeah, let's do this. I'll pull up next spring on the calendar." He walked to his office and then returned to the table. "Early April's looking good. Is that too soon?"

Five months away. He'd have to work like a mofo to make all the pieces fit by then.

"Let's shake on it."

"Great Bo, happy to do business with you. I'm going to send Stef a little text and give him the heads-up about Sunday. That was when you were planning on coming by, right?" Jesse was reading his mind.

"How did you guess?"

CHAPTER 56

The week dragged until Friday lazily made its appearance. No shenanigans at work, Margret's week had been fine, and now it was almost time to find out the fate of his CD.

He crammed every possible chore into Saturday and then asked Margret if she wanted to walk on the boardwalk on Coney Island. It took a bus trip to the opposite end of Brooklyn and it was the perfect way to end the day. There were not many rides open in November but there were always the bumper cars and storefront fortune tellers. They indulged themselves on the rich culinary offerings of the neighborhood like Nathan's franks and French fries. They walked two blocks to the boardwalk and almost got hit by a speeding bicyclist. The sun was starting to go down and the chill made Margret zip up her jacket.

"I'm impressed. A real date," she said, leaning into him. "Why haven't we done this sooner?"

Bo put his arm around her. "I don't know, but let's do more of this. Thanks for helping me keep my mind off tomorrow. Are you ready to go home?"

Margret nodded.

"I'm setting two alarms for the morning, but can you be the third? Make sure I'm up by 6. I need to get ready to make my dream pitch."

"What if we stay up all night? I know how we can keep busy."

"I bet you do."

CHAPTER 57

Rising a half hour before his alarms went off, Bo got ready and told Margret he was going into the city early. "I'll grab a paper and get some coffee at a diner," he said, kissing her goodbye.

The subway took him four blocks away from The Minor Seventh. He walked in the opposite direction and, the next block over, found a place to kill some time.

At fifteen minutes after eight, not wanting to jump on Stef Dalton the moment he walked in, Bo left a five-dollar bill on the counter and walked to the club. The old bassist was already there, in a back corner facing the front door. He saw Bo approaching and gave him a wide smile.

"Good morning, Mr. Dalton, I'm Bo," he said, hand extended briskly.

The man dabbed a napkin to his lips. "Please, my friend, you need to call me Stef." Bo had been corrected, but it was done with warmth. "Yes, *Stef*, of course! So good to see you again – that is, if you remember me."

"I surely do. Jesse told me you'd be stopping by. I don't get too many visitors at breakfast anymore," he said, recalling a time when his peers were still alive.

"What's this about a new project?" he asked. "I'm always down to get into some trouble." A faint smile was followed by a sip of his milky coffee.

Stef pushed his plate away. On it were two half-bitten triangles of toasted rye. Unopened butters were scattered in front of him. Ever since his sixties, the appetite wasn't what it used to be. There was a brush with prostate cancer, and with the little walnut-shaped gland zapped into nonexistence by radiation, he wasn't so hungry anymore.

"Well." *How to start?*

"I've been on a personal family-roots kind of journey. There's no other way to say it. And from that, I've decided that I want to make a CD with all-original music that lets the listener feel what I've felt, the full range of emotions."

So far, so good: Stef was following along. His brown eyes had yellowed with age and his lids sagged, but there was a spark when he heard the words *family roots*. "Tell me more."

"Two months ago, I made an incredible discovery about a piece of music that's part of my family lineage. It turns out that we had a great-great uncle on my dad's side who was enslaved on a plantation. He was a musician. That's what they say."

Stef nodded slowly. "What kind of musician? How do you know this?"

It wasn't the best time to choke up, but Stef would understand. Bo's eyes watered and he continued.

"My Gramma used to sing this song to us about a bird that takes flight. Her wing's broken and she's starving. But she soars anyway. She told us it came from this far-back uncle, Lymus Jefferson Abbott. He was a pianist, a poet, maybe a singer, so I'm told. He lived and died a slave." Bo knew what was coming next.

"Sing it for me."

Bo shifted in his seat and scooted a little closer to Stef. "Okay. I'm filling in some words because I can't be sure my memory is straight on all this. But here goes." Bo hummed a few bars and then sang softly.

The bird is full of hope;

She tends to her young.

When life gets hard

When she is torn up

She gets stronger.

She will fly to her duty

She will love with her whole heart

This bird, one bird. Full of hope.

Silence followed as Stef gently tapped on his coffee cup. "Waitress?" He turned around to the kitchen, looking for her. She headed over to the table. "Can you refresh my cup?" he asked.

Bo waited patiently for a reaction. He had just spilled out his ancestral guts. It was nerve-wracking. He was afraid Stef would say it sounded contrived, made up. How could anybody remember what a slave had sung?

Stef hummed a few bars quietly. "Yeah. I like it. I'll tell you why." The waitress came over to top him off, and with a small smile at both men left them to their conversation.

"Long time ago I did this piece with ascending fourths," Stef began. "I improvised some really good shit around it. I mean, that wasn't unusual, but what was strange was it made me cry." He shook his head, remembering. "Well, the audience really dug it. Let me tell you, it had this weird, cold feel, kind of like 'Keiko and the Lavender Moon' if you know the song."

"Actually, I heard it on Sesame Street, of all things. I know the feeling you mean."

"So," Stef continued. "Here I am standing in a corner of the stage, almost against the back wall, where there's this narrow walkway to my right. The waitstaff would come behind us, actually on stage, to get to some of the customers at the far end of the club. But it's not like they were hidden, I mean, people could see the waiters frantically navigating the space with plates piled up and drinks on platters and so on. You catch my drift."

Bo nodded.

"And because they kept crisscrossing their way back and forth, I felt compelled to create something really different, to get the audience's attention, because one of them, this Spanish waiter, he was a little flashily dressed and way too handsome for my tastes. I mean, he distracted the audience, right?"

"I'm following you." Bo was eating this up.

"The solos came 'round and it was my turn at the till. The ascending fourths just jumped into my brain. I worked and worried those strings for a long time. Maybe it wasn't thoughtful to take up so much time, so much bandwidth, not trading off yet with the other cats, but on I went, plying my strings and just going up and up..."

Stef sipped at his coffee but it was still steaming hot. He jerked his face away and grunted. "Do they get this straight from the sun or something? Damn!" He poured in lots of cream and continued.

"Suddenly, from the kitchen, this little New York City sparrow comes bee-lining his way in and makes a loop right around my head. I swear. Here I am workin' the fretboard until I reach the bridge, and then, damned if I didn't plink past it to the very ends of the strings. I went as far as I could." *Beyond the Bridge*; what a great title for a song. Bo banked the idea.

"I love the visuals here," Bo said. "Do you think my Gramma's song ties into this?"

"Yeah, fool! And I say that lovingly. Course it does. But I was thinking something else," said Stef. "The bird, well, he went as far as he could. Let me tell you, there's a big industrial ceiling fan way up there. Remember, this place is O-L-D, old! Authentic tin ceiling tiles, greasy and grimy as hell. This fella almost gets scooped into the maelstrom of air going 'round the fan blades. He gets his own little strength going, though, and pulls himself out, into the kitchen again, and out the back door."

Stef's feathered friend went beyond his own bridge...perhaps only by way of anecdote, which may or may not be true. You never knew with Stef.

"Your Gramma's song out-and-out reminds me of that night," said Stef. "You like the fourths? You like the soaring, hopeful vibe?"

"I'm loving everything about it," Bo replied. "Do you – would you want to compose something around it? Do you feel like we should keep Lymus's lyrics?" *Did I just spill the beans and ask my mentor to collaborate with me? Have I lost my damn mind?*

"I have some holes in my schedule." Stef chuckled, which turned into a more rigorous guffaw, complete with a slap on the table. "These clubs here, they want to feature the emerging talent, not us old folks, and that's totally cool with me. But there's so many of them, and I go to bed early anyway. So occasionally I'll sit in, but mostly I've given them the floor. Their turn."

It wasn't bitterness. It was good-natured generosity tinged with nostalgia for his younger days.

"So yeah, it'll be fun. Let's do it. And your bass too, man. We need two bass lines, so you better get to writing it."

Bo thought he needed to get his hearing checked. It sounded like Stef wanted to collaborate on a song, not just writing it together, but playing it together. He was stunned.

How would this work? He couldn't afford to pay Stef for his time. He didn't know how to unspool the conversation.

"I'd give my left arm to work with you, but I have zero funds to back that up. I didn't mean to jump to conclusions."

"I can't jump anymore, that's for sure." Stef grinned. "But writin' down some notes, meeting new musicians, taking a few hours of studio time to get you an audio file, yeah man, this crusty guy can still do that."

Bo was speechless.

"Before you say any more, I don't want to be paid. I'll sign something for ya, here, put it on the napkin and I'll sign, right now." He got a kick out of Bo's bewildered look. "Now you got me all about this thing so don't be changing your mind."

"Never – no – you for real about the napkin?"

"Of course I am. But you better not give me one red cent. Call it a labor of love. Call it tryin' to stay relevant. Fuck my agent, she doesn't have to know."

"Okay then! To screwing your agent!" Bo raised his coffee mug. Stef raised his and they tapped them together.

"As long as you don't mind naming the song," Stef said.

What was happening? This was so off-script that Bo thought he must be dreaming.

"My whole career, I've always hated that part, the naming. What would you call it?" Stef asked.

Think fast and don't screw up. "Okay, so when you were talking about that bird and what you were doing musically, I was thinking *Beyond the Bridge,*" Bo said.

"I'm feeling it. Okay then, that's the title," said Stef. "Also, I hear a vocalist. Or better yet, some spoken word threaded between some hot, silky vocals." Stef was beaming now. Bo had a sheen of sweat on his face from the excitement of things to come.

"Bo, how about you write the bones of it, the chord changes, and I'll take care of the melody based on what you sang to me. And that poetry from Lymus, man, that will work like a hand in a glove. I know this great singer from Manhattan, and she's on fire right now. She owes me one."

The light in Stef's eyes burned brighter. No doubt there was a story there.

CHAPTER 58

Bo came crashing through the door, keys jangling a bebop tune. He was all smiles.

"I guess it went poorly," Margret teased.

"Poorly indeed, my love, poorly enough for him to be in like Flynn!" Bo said giddily.

Margret threw her arms around him and offered up a loud smooch. "I knew you'd convince him. How could he say no to such a cute punim?" Every so often she pulled out the Yiddish to keep him on his toes.

"I made some chili, hon. Come take a sniff, but no tastes 'til dinnertime." Margret flumped into the loveseat hugging a body pillow and patted the cushion next to her. "Tell me everything he said and how you closed the deal."

The unwavering enthusiasm over one another's triumphs was at the heart of their love affair. Bo knew he was living a very rare life.

"Smells amazing. I'm taking some, just a spoonful, because you're torturing me." He stuck a spoon in the pot and sipped. "Mmm! Babe, even better than last time and that was a total grand slam."

"Sit and talk, Bo. I can't believe he's going to play with you. Will you rehearse together or just send him some sheet music?"

Margret must be thinking of the 1980s.

"No, and the last thing I want to do is impose on his limited time. I'll make a rough video of me playing a few chords on the piano to outline it and basically narrating what'll go where. You know, hi hats, brushes, sax and so on." Bo was a functional pianist, enough to be able to compose and arrange, but nothing more. The video would convey enough information for Stef to riff off that.

"This has the potential to be press-worthy," he continued. "I'd love for the guy to get some media attention. He deserves it for his lifetime contribution to jazz. I mean, you're a champ your whole career and then you just fade into oblivion? That's not right."

CHAPTER 59

Bo spent the next few hours watching videos of Stef's performances over the years. There was an old interview of him on Johnny Carson and also the Mike Douglas show, and footage from festivals and concerts in Europe, Japan and Scandinavia. But that was long ago. This man should be on Trevor Noah and Colbert and SNL, thought Bo. The masses need to be re-educated on jazz. Not enough of that going around!

The chili was soon just a memory. Margret was about to pull up a Liam Neeson movie on Netflix. It was terribly tempting, but Bo couldn't wait to get into his music room and start composing "Beyond the Bridge."

"No movie for me, sorry, hon. I'm all fresh from my meeting with Stef. I'll make it up to ya…"

Margret put a folded bag of popcorn into the microwave and pressed a button. "Just me and Liam, then. We're not waiting for you."

"You are simply the best," said Bo.

"Don't forget it."

After three hours – way past Liam's inevitable triumph over evil – Bo reappeared into the living room, a smile on his face. It was time to let Stef take a listen to the song. Bo thought it sounded pretty good, but the master would definitely elevate it. It was too late to call him, and Bo hoped the text wouldn't wake him up either.

Hey Stef, how's it going? I'm about to send you the private Soundcloud link to what I laid down on keys for "Beyond the Bridge." It's roughly hewn, as they say, but you'll get where I'm going, I'm sure. I'm loving F major for this. – Bo

As he waited to hear back from Stef on the song's bare bones, he went back to his keyboard and played it more slowly, filling in with arpeggios, improvising on the theme, and listening for where Lymus's words would fit in. So relentlessly did the song begin to haunt him that he felt the poetry flowing through his fingertips, channeling Lymus.

Bo imagined ideas of hope and freedom that must have both plagued and inspired Lymus for all his days, particularly when he went off into the woods scented by magnolia petals at his feet, and wrote his songs. The ground was sun-dappled with light finding its way between the branches, yet the substantial tree trunks provided enough privacy for an optimistic scribe with music in his soul.

Had he survived to live a full and free life, he might have written more amazing music; might have flown with his own wings, like Icarus, towards the sun, but this time returning safely home.

CHAPTER 60

It had been weeks since Bo heard from Zack, and he wasn't holding out much hope. Immersing himself in the CD was an excellent distraction.

"Sorry for the delay, Bo. You might have guessed by now that there's a statute of limitations on your great-great uncle's situation," Zack told him.

"Even though I know in my bones that the melody was lifted from the producer and his wife?" Bo felt a nagging annoyance returning by the prickle from underneath his shirt collar.

"I hear you. But it would be hard to prove, definitively, that they came into contact with the music and that they ripped it off. And like I said, the case is just too old, my friend."

Bo's chest deflated. "There's no precedent anywhere?"

"Not really." Zack recalled a case involving an old folk tune. It was from a different time period and happened in Romania. "But there's some context. You're not the first person to think a black man from Lymus's generation or shortly after had their music ripped off."

"Like who?" Bo asked.

"Well, Scott Joplin accused Irving Berlin of stealing his music. That went basically nowhere. Jelly Roll Morton was called paranoid in some circles. He was convinced everyone was plagiarizing him."

"You know your jazz history," said Bo.

"Well, you give me a task and I'm on it. Even if I'm delayed. Oh, and then there was the time Pete Seeger wanted to copyright 'We Shall Overcome' and a whole lot of noise started up about its origins and if anybody owned it."

Bo perked up. "How far did that get?"

"It started as a gospel hymn that was composed by a Philadelphia reverend. It caught on like fire. Everyone from people in the civil rights sphere to tobacco pickers to ministers and even Eastern Europeans in the Cold War used a variation of it. Around 1960, Seeger wanted to copyright it, finding it was the perfect protest song, but two music publishers owned the copyright."

"Seems complicated," Bo noted.

"Precisely. Then a new suit came up a few years ago arguing the song should be in the public domain. What I'm saying here is that not only is the statute exhausted, the road is long and ultimately difficult if not impossible to prove."

It didn't look good. "Now what?"

"Not sure if there's anything else to be done. Nobody's alive from that time – obviously, former slaves, the plantation owner – and these entertainment folks, they all died by the 1990s. Except the Fettermans, of course. But there's nothing to hang your hat on to actually sue them. Sorry, Bo."

Bo closed his eyes, trying to imagine Lymus writing his songs in secret, afraid of the beating that would follow if he was discovered. "Yeah, I got it," he said slowly. "Thanks for being there for me. I just feel I need to bring it out into the open somehow. If only to give it the respect it finally deserves."

Zack formed a small smile on his face, which of course Bo couldn't see on the phone. He loved his friend and was proud he held to his convictions.

That evening, Bo considered his composition skills. They were just shy of mediocre. The couple of songs he'd already written for the CD might not make it to any big festivals or concert halls. Regardless, it was time to give Lymus Abbott his due.

CHAPTER 61

"Hey Mags." Bo was watching his sweetheart emerge from a steamy shower. There was no time for marital antics, but he always admired how she kept in shape despite the stress of her career and the God-awful food choices in the hospital cafeteria. She looked fresh as a new-sprung daisy and was sexy to boot.

"Yah? You rang?" She slid past him as she toweled off her arms and legs.

"I was thinking about how this is all going to work, all the personal dynamics between the four of us, when we used to play together. I'm a little on edge."

"Wait, how what's going to work?"

"You remember what happened between Pip and Joey with that Tina girl? They couldn't stand being near each other because of that. I hope they've both let bygones be bygones and they can participate on the CD like mature adults."

Sleepy Tina – now an investment banker whose vocal cords had lost their memory of The Great American Songbook – had been a pot-loving hanger-on when they played in college and both Pip and Joey were crazy about her. She sang a few songs and had an incredible voice but she was very unreliable and forgot to show for gigs. She pulled herself out of their orbit after they all graduated and didn't stay in touch. They had heard she married the founder of a tech startup which was on its way to replicating the success of Google and Yahoo. It would be a stretch to think Tina could even remember these scruffy musicians who fought over her.

"Did you want to try to bring her on?" Margret asked.

"No, not at all! Perish the thought. Besides, Stef mentioned he has a vocalist he wanted us to check out. I'm still waiting to get her contact info."

History was about to repeat itself.

CHAPTER 62

The vocalist I told you about, Chanel, has a free and short window of opportunity. She's gonna contact you asap so get her up to speed w Beyond the Bridge. Trust me when I say she has a knack for weaving spoken word. Already sent you my suggestions on the song but it's pretty good as is. Anyway - be ready!

Stef's text came through the very next morning and Bo knew more than to waste Stef's time asking questions. He nearly jumped out of bed.

"What's up? So eager to get to work?" Margret asked him. Normally he gave himself a half hour in the mornings to make coffee, catch up on his socials and lounge a bit before getting ready for work.

"Stef sent my info to Chanel, the girl who's going to sing on that one track. I got the feeling this is a special person to him, either past or present."

"Is the song ready for her?" Margret asked, starting the shower. She set her coffee cup on the dresser and slipped out of her robe.

"Pretty much. I already booked the studio time. Fritz is supposed to meet us there next weekend. She'll be coming from uptown, according to Stef."

"How's she going to get enough time to practice it before you record?"

"Stef said she's on her game. This whole project has some crazy deadlines, but we have to make it all work to release on time in April."

Steam leaked out of the shower into the hallway. "Joining me?"

Just then, Bo's phone buzzed.

"Bad timing. It's a text from Chanel. Can I just – "

"Raincheck, yup."

She blew a kiss and closed the shower door after her.

CHAPTER 63

It was easy to put out feelers about his new album on social media, and having just opened an Instagram account, he posted a teaser: "Upcoming CD coming soon from Bo Abbott Quartet inspired by a personal journal of my family history." With no artwork yet to accompany it, he used a copyright-free image of a bassist whose face had been blurred, reminding him to stop procrastinating and get the collateral materials designed.

He looked around at some of the photographers and illustrators and found Talia Seaford. He loved her images. They were eye-catching and looked fresh. It turned out she had designed over 100 CD covers for musicians in the UK, Denmark, South Africa and Russia. Hers was an eclectic portfolio. She also did corporate work for big conglomerates, social service organizations and even designed two pieces for the government of Israel.

Bo loved her use of color and mixed media combined with inventive typefaces, many of them imposed on black and white photos which was very much his design sensibility. Although the great majority of her CD artwork was for rock albums, Bo could see beyond that. Her designs felt just right for his CD.

Talia had a huge Instagram platform – tens of thousands of followers. Bo wondered if her costs would be out of reach. She didn't post her rates. There was no way to know unless he asked *her*.

CONTACT ME – fill out the information below and let's talk!

NAME: Bo Abbott

SUBJECT: CD cover design

MESSAGE: Hi Talia, I saw your work on Insta and love your designs. We have a jazz CD coming out in April and I was wondering if we could talk. Please email me, thanks a bunch!

He hit send and then drifted over to the kitchen.

"Hey baby." Margret was washing peppers for a huge salad. She'd just cut a handful of fresh basil and the kitchen smelled deliciously peppery. "Jersey tomatoes on the way?"

"You know it." She turned to kiss him.

"I was just wondering about the budget. I found this artist I want to use for the cover art. I have no idea of her fees. What do you think we can afford for this? It can be tax deductible if I list it as a work expense."

She rubbed her nose with the side of her hand, holding onto the scraper. Carrots figured big in the Abbott household. "Well that is, if we itemize. But first off, what are you thinking would be doable? I have no idea how much these things go for."

Somebody like Talia Seaford might command a high price for her work. He had nothing to lose by trying, but the budget was always tight. They rented an apartment in Brooklyn, and that was the majority of their monthly nut.

"Turning the question back on me. I see how it is." He poked her. She dropped the scraper onto the counter.

"Bo, stop!"

He nuzzled her neck. "I've seen info about all kinds of prices. From a few hundred for a small band like ours to five or ten thousand."

"On the high end? We can't afford that."

"I know. I'll just see what she comes up with. But the vocalist, Chanel McGhee – it's 'Shanny' to her friends – isn't charging us a fee. I don't know what favors Stef called in but she's on board for nada."

"How did that come about?" Margret asked.

"I think they had something going on. Maybe they still do."

CHAPTER 64

The ER intake desk had become nothing less than 24/7 chaos. It was wintertime in the Northeast and everybody knew that meant car accidents, slip and falls, and lots of respiratory illnesses.

Bo made the mistake (as he soon learned) of telling Aimee about his upcoming CD. He'd decided in the name of getting along and moving past that uncomfortable night at the club to move on to more positive subjects.

Aimee was thrilled to find out that Stef was going to be a guest musician on it, a development she took credit for. (Bo didn't really thank her properly, and though he didn't know it yet, he'd have his chance.) There was very little time for chitchat, though, because the registration reps were flying all over the place trying to get to the patients before they were whisked off for X-rays for broken bones or chest congestion.

First shift was almost over. Second shift reps were clocking in and putting their dinners in the dorm-sized refrigerator in the office. Bo greeted the fresh-faced staff and smiled at their more haggard counterparts who were waiting to go home for the day. Aimee managed to look great no matter what the ER brought. That was problem one.

Problem two was that Aimee called him into the hallway. She was holding something in a plastic bag that looked like a book. "Bo, do you have just a second?"

It was a corner of the hallway right past the elevators. Most employees from the ER didn't use this elevator bank. His uh-oh response dinged.

"Hi Aimee. I got about three seconds, literally. What's up?"

"I found this book in the remainder bin and thought you might have use for it. It's about marketing for musicians. It's pretty new so I have no idea why it wasn't on the regular shelves."

Aimee obviously wanted to have more of a conversation, but Bo had no time for it.

"Thank you – you shouldn't have, and as your boss," he straightened up and smiled, "I really shouldn't accept this, but I will because, well, thanks." He was rambling and realized this was taking more than three seconds.

"Do you have the release date yet? I really want to go." *Aha. That's the reason for this private convo.*

Bo cleared his throat and looked over to the office. Second shift was streaming out with their COWs. A trauma was announced on the audio system. "I can get you and Matt seats, sure. Just to let you know, it's a fundraiser for the wife of the club owner who's pretty sick, so donations are welcomed. I get a very small fraction of the door, enough to pay the musicians." He really had to go.

"Oh. Matt. Yeah, I'll ask him." She didn't sound convincing. Bo was determined to treat her as part of a couple. He was done letting her control the narrative.

"Great. No date yet, spring to be sure. Have a good evening!"

He left her in what looked like mid-sentence. She would get her pound of flesh, though.

CHAPTER 65

Shanny – she used "Chanel" as a stage name – was waiting at the studio when Bo arrived out of breath. "I am so sorry," he said, sticking his hand out. "You must be Stef's friend." Bo wasn't sure how to navigate that. "I'm –" Shanny didn't hesitate to respond. "I know, Bo, the boy wonder. Or so says Stef."

A small blush came over him, not only at the thought of being regarded with such a moniker by the great Stef Dalton, but also because he got a whiff of what seemed to be oranges, and it struck him as very lovely. As was this young woman.

And so what?

"I appreciate you for coming down here on such short notice," he said. "I know time is tight and the clock is ticking, so shall we start? It was crazy booking some time here, they're so jammed."

Shanny watched Bo unzip the cover of his bass, peel it off and fold it up inside where the wheels were attached. "Stef has a good ear for when my input is needed, and I always listen to him," she said. "I also went on YouTube to look up your band but I didn't find anything."

"Well, I'm a dinosaur," he said. "Nothing pre-internet. It was back in our college days and I thank God for that, because our playing was pretty awful. But we had a lot of fun doing it."

Shanny stretched her neck from side to side and did a few breathing exercises to warm up. "I bet you had a pretty good groove. Still got it, you think?"

"We'll see." Bo smiled politely.

He took out his bow and tightened it, blowing gently along the synthetic hair to remove the extra rosin. It made a white puff. He then hummed a middle A and double-checked it against his phone app. He tuned his strings up and down and back again, trying to zero in on the right note. The interval between the notes on an upright bass were gargantuan. It took a sophisticated ear to bring all the strings into their rightful places.

He looked over at Shanny. "We weren't going to use vocals, but Stef kind of insisted." She pouted at this, wondering if she was really needed here. If not, why did she waste an afternoon trekking downtown to this tiny studio in yet another cookie-cutter hipster neighborhood?

"No, I don't mean that in a bad way," Bo said. "I was looking for an all-instrumental sound in the beginning, but I had no idea how fortune would smile upon me and deliver the one and only Mr. Dalton. Then he told us about bringing you on the album. I can flow with that," he said cheerfully.

"Stef definitely talked you up," he continued. "I saw some of your online videos. Your voice is amazing.

Charismatic, strong." Bo was talking too much. It was his small terror of beautiful women.

When Shanny adjusted her mic, he noticed she wasn't wearing a ring. Then he remembered Stef's sparkle when he mentioned her. He wondered if she and Stef were still involved, even though he was married to the same woman for over 50 years. *Not my business. As long as the CD gets made.*

Bo's phone vibrated with a text from Joey: *OMW, dont start w/o moi.* "That was my drummer," he said to Shanny. "Don't worry, he's on the way, and he's also a master of the quick set-up."

"Okay, then, why don't we practice a little before he gets here? Every minute counts." Her mic was ready. Bo cued the backing track.

"How about I play the head a few times around, then you come in with your vocals?" he asked. She nodded.

Bo had sent Shanny and Joey the same music file he sent to Stef, outlining "Beyond the Bridge." Joey barely looked at it and sent back two small suggestions. But Shanny ran with it and was now belting out a brand-new subtext of the theme, describing the little bird's migration halfway around the world and its ultimate disappointment in not finding a place to call home. This was going to be reflected in Stef's climb up the fretboard and dramatically dropping down fifth by fifth until he plucked each string, ending on the lowest possible note.

They were doing a raw take just to see how the song laid out. In the ninth measure when Bo nodded for her to come in, a pure, clear sound filled the studio. It sent goosebumps coursing up his arms. He needed those arms to play his instrument. Hearing her sing was like listening to cascading waves of bells. Her phrasing was impeccable, employing a slight pull-back from the rhythm to give the impression of lagging that fit the song perfectly.

Bo knew immediately how impactful this song was going to be. Right then and there he pegged it as the standout track of the CD. Even his most personal songs, the one about Lymus and the one written for Margret, would pale in comparison.

Go with it, he told himself. Unify with the music. Stay inside it.

They didn't notice when Joey came in until he dropped a finger cymbal that dinged loudly on the floor and rolled in circles before coming to a stop. "Sorry!" he stage-whispered.

Bo stopped playing and laughed deeply. "Hey Fritzy, my man! Great to see you!"

"You must be Chanel?" Joey asked, trying not to look like a wolf among sheep.

"That I am, but please call me Shanny." She smiled at him, then gave Bo a wink.

Bo and Shanny resumed the song. Joey quickly set up his kit, the mic in position. He had practiced the song a few times and was more than ready to factor in the layer of vocals. However, he wasn't ready to be swept away by the young woman singing them.

Joey had no idea he was about to repeat his own dysfunctional history.

CHAPTER 66

The full story of what happened between Tina and Joey was never explained to Bo, who didn't have a head for drama. One night when Bo and Pip were talking on the phone about the order of songs on the CD, Pip brought it up. He was obviously no fan of Joey's and thought Bo should know who they were dealing with. Bo was about to find out how weird the situation had become.

Years ago, when they were all young collegiates, Pip had fallen madly and abruptly in love with Tina. It was instant, faster than a finger snap. He found her wandering the streets at Pace University, an urban campus in Manhattan with a few unlikely trees and slightly more space between buildings than normally found in New York.

She was obviously stoned. But beyond the vapid state of personal relinquishment there was something about her that pulled him in.

He found out she was a language major (Italian, which she was not, only the first of her many mysteries). She sang on the side to make a little money, which was immediately handed over to anyone on campus selling weed. When she wasn't high, actually when she was high, too, she talked of a career on Broadway, off-Broadway or in cabarets. She didn't care exactly where, but she loved singing and was damn good at it. She had an effortless voice, almost weightless, the embodiment of an ice skater etching intricate patterns without trying.

Pip, Joey, Bo and Tim were friends since high school and into college. Pip was the only one to stay downtown for his undergraduate studies. Bo hiked up to City College in the Bronx, Tim did his Associates in physics at Kingsborough in Brooklyn and then decided to concentrate on his music, and Joey took up ethnomusicology at Rutgers in New Jersey. They still got together nearly every weekend and looked for gigs.

When Pip told the guys about meeting Tina and how she sounded like 'an angel on fire' they knew it was all over. "You're going to ask her out?" asked Joey. He had a bad track record when it came to dating and was on the receiving end of several ugly breakups by women who called him "intense." If he was about to give some advice on the topic of romance, his friends knew to humor him but then disregard whatever he said and do the exact opposite.

"Of course I am," said Pip, grinning. "It doesn't hurt that she has good weed too."

"Oh yeah, right," said Bo, rolling his eyes. "Let's not forget that, which is exactly what I look for in a suitable mate." Pip laughed, then told him to shut up.

The four guys practiced wherever they could find a rehearsal room – sometimes traveling to Jersey to get into Rutgers on Joey's ID, sometimes to Pace – and soon developed a functional, decent sound. Local bars that lost their house band or had last-minute cancellations would call Bo, who everybody agreed was the most organized. He managed everybody's schedules, made sure they rehearsed new songs and got to their gigs on time. This was not an easy feat when marijuana was involved.

Tina often showed up at rehearsals as she and Pip became more serious. Joey couldn't understand why she'd go for him. Pip acted silly around her and Joey felt he jumped at her every wish. Once at a gig near Pace she supposedly forgot her wallet and when Bo offered her a subway token to get home, she replied that she didn't want to ride the train alone at night. Pip drew out a few grimy bills from his wallet and put her in a cab back to Brooklyn. "She's walking all over you, man," Joey said. "I hope you make her pay you back." Pip's eyes flashed at him. "What do you care?" he asked.

As the semester wore on, Joey kept bringing up Tina in conversation which started to annoy Pip. "You have a thing for my girl or something?" he asked. Joey narrowed his eyes. "Well, she's smokin' hot and all, but she has you wrapped around her little finger. I mean, if that's your thing." "Stick to your drums, man," Pip said. Things were going too well with the band for there to be any in-fighting. He did his best to let these incidents pass.

One night before a gig while they were setting up their equipment on stage, Tina went outside to have a cigarette. Joey stepped out for a puff too. This was a good excuse to chat with her before the set began.

"How's it going, Sleepy Tina?" he said, leaning back against the brick ledge in front of the club that she was sitting on. He was just a few inches away from her bare legs (she looked amazing in cutoffs). He fought the urge to run his hand over her calf.

"Really, don't call me that," she pouted. "It's the weed that makes me relax and all. But I'm not sleepy."

"Oh no? Then what are you?" Joey was great at rolls and cut-time but had no sense for repartee, especially with a woman he was attracted to. It made no difference that she was Pip's girlfriend.

"Actually, I'm quite sharp and aware. Ask Pip, he knows." She drew on her cigarette. That was a little mean, Joey thought. But then she laughed, and it sounded like chimes. So pretty.

"Well you could've fooled me," he said. Then, sensing time was almost out – he could hear Bo tuning his strings and saying "Yeah, that's the place" – Joey put his hand out, just for a second, and patted her calf, moving it up and down her leg, just a little.

Tina jumped off the ledge, scraping the back of her thighs. "You freaking creepster! Stay the hell away from me, asshole." She threw the rest of her cigarette on the ground and stubbed it out with her sandal. Joey heard the door swing open and then slam shut.

Tina told Pip what had happened immediately after their last set, but for the sake of keeping the band together and because Pip had not yet grown into his own empowerment, he again let this pass. He kept an eye out for Joey but tried not to let it affect their flow on stage.

Then things got worse.

Joey thought they should be playing more original material and began writing songs that he wanted them to play. Songs with lyrics. This was not at all surprising because it was clear he wanted to get Tina up on stage with them.

Things became even more uncomfortable.

Joey had found her address on the back cover of Pip's song book and decided to send her a letter. It was a very bizarre letter. It didn't profess love or lust like a normal but immature young man might write. Instead, it was filled with lists and sentence fragments describing how she might look in different styles of clothing with drawings of her wearing them. Every drawing showed her with heavy lidded eyes. It was signed 'Your not-so-secret admirer, Joey.' He was obviously a few matches short of a matchbook.

Tina knew he was attracted to her but she couldn't believe he had sent her a letter, which she thought was probably going to be a poem or song lyrics. When she opened it and saw the sketches of herself, she freaked out and told Pip she couldn't take it anymore. Either he had to tell Joey to back the hell off or she was going to take the next exit.

Pip couldn't bear the thought of losing Tina but he was also afraid of breaking up the band. He knew he had to do something. He had to make a choice.

He chose love.

The band broke up the next day, but Pip had never discussed the letter with anybody. Bo and Tim only knew about Joey being a flirt and just thought it had come to a boiling point.

It fell on Bo to get them out of the gigs that were in the works, and he didn't like doing it. He knew he was burning future bridges. Pip was understandably furious about the whole thing, and Bo and Tim were disgusted with Joey's behavior. They knew they couldn't play with him anymore.

Pip went off to repair whatever damage had been done. He and Tina stayed together a few years and eventually broke up but remained friends. He moved to Boston for a change of scenery, got his teacher's license and became a tenured professor. He gave private lessons on the side and took occasional studio work.

Joey went off on his own, finding fill-in gigs and gaining a rep as a weird but very talented drummer. He came up with an idea for a better drumstick (it was weighted inside with different materials, making it easier to play) which he sold to a major manufacturer for substantial cash. His girlfriend at the time, Lesslie, brought him to Costa Rica to raise money for the stray dogs there. He stopped playing music to have more time to explore his new island life which included stalking young women. Lesslie found out and moved back to her parents' home in Ohio.

Why Bo decided to involve Joey in their new CD was a mystery to Margret as well as Pip and Tim, but Bo felt there was magic to be made. Joey was quite frankly the best drummer Bo knew. He was about to find out that Joey hadn't changed his stripes at all, and it would put their CD in jeopardy.

CHAPTER 67

Your little drummer boy, he's a problem. Shanny might want out. Better come quick, my friend.

The ominous text from Stef instantly raised Bo's blood pressure a few points. What went down and why wasn't he aware of it before it became an issue?

First I'm hearing of it. Sorry to hear! Will get on it asap. Tell Shanny to please hold on.

Bo walked into the tiny sunlit dining room where Margret breathed in the aroma from a cup of chai latte she'd made herself. The Starbucks version was too sweet.

"Well, looks like Joey has struck again. Damage control time. I can't believe this."

Margret looked up from her laptop where she had been reading the Radiology Professional newsletter. "What the heck?"

Bo pulled on a blue t-shirt over his impressive physique. "He did something to piss off Shanny. And she's an integral part of the CD. Not only because of her vocals, but -"

She finished the thought. "Because of your relationship with Stef. What a mess. I wonder what he did. I can only imagine."

"Oh, you can imagine. I've told you about him and Tina. I just hope it's not beyond fixing."

Bo thought very carefully about the words he was about to text. *Shanny, I just heard from Stef - something about Joey. Can we please meet to talk about it? I'll come uptown.*

Shanny had been waiting for his text. Stef told her to cool her heels until Bo could set things right. She responded quickly.

Sure. But just know that I am not going to be in the same room as Joey's sorry ass ever again.

Bo suggested that they meet at Andrew's Diner on the Upper West Side at noon.

"I'm going to give myself an hour and a half to get up there. Do you mind? Wanna come with?" he asked Margret.

"No, not a chance. Where Joey's concerned, I'm happy to stay out of it."

CHAPTER 68

Shanny took a booth in the back of the diner. She had ordered a double chocolate chip muffin. As skinny as she was, she loved carbs more than life itself. She'd walk the twenty-two blocks home to work some of it off.

Bo came in with barely a smile. He told himself to slow his pace. It would be best to keep the discussion relaxed. Just two friends with a common interest.

She stood and put out her hand. "So official!" he said. His smile came easier. "Thanks for meeting me on such short notice."

"That's fine. One thing about Andrew's is their muffins are on point."

Bo wasn't about to study the menu. He told the waitress he wanted a cup of black coffee with a blueberry muffin.

"First, before you tell me what happened, I wanted to make sure to thank you for being on the CD and meeting us downtown to record the song. It was an amazing afternoon." Bo felt the moisture underneath his pits. Not a good look.

"The pleasure was mine," she said. "I think we killed it. I can't wait until the CD comes out." Had she really said that? Maybe it wasn't a lost cause.

Bo looked straight at her. "Now, Joey. He has a history with women, so I hope whatever happened wasn't too severe. Did you want to share it?"

She took a long, slow breath, closed her eyes, and let it out. "Oh yeah. I have no shyness about it. Your guy, he's a pig." She put the period on it. Bo wasn't about to push her.

Shanny took a sip of her green tea, too hot and almost burning her lips. With striking hazel eyes, a perfect smile and skin that was crystal clear, she was not only beautiful but smart and talented too. No wonder there seemed to be a little something between Stef and her. Bo would be patient and let her say what happened when she was ready.

"Suffice to say, I almost called to tell you I was out of this album." One more bite of the muffin. She could certainly put it away. Where, was another story. Her body was taut and muscular. She must run, thought Bo.

"I'm all ears."

"Okay. So after the studio, Joey walked me out and we started walking in the same direction. I thought he was going to grab the subway or New Jersey Transit or something. Then I found out he drove. He was parked right near the studio and asked if I wanted a lift."

Oh no. He made a pass at her in the car?

"He asked me if he could give me a lift home. I didn't want this guy to know where I live so I said okay, take me up to the northern end of the park."

They were fortunate to live close to their respective parks in the city, Bo near Prospect Park in Brooklyn and Shanny near the more sprawling Central Park in Manhattan. She would have to take a short bus ride home from there, but she was trying not to be rude to Joey.

Shanny continued. "There was a lot of traffic and I was nervous about being in the car with him, but Stef vetted you for me and by proxy I thought Joey would be a decent guy too. But I was obviously wrong. Soon as we got to the West Side Highway, he started asking me weird questions. I think he was talking about some chick named Tina and asking why did I think she wouldn't like his poems, or something."

Bo had recalled Pip telling him about the letter. It was a stupid move on Joey's part, to be followed by even dumber behaviors bordering on stalkerish.

"I'm so sorry. That jerk had no business bothering you. He should have said 'nice meeting you' and been on his merry way back to Jersey." The acid forming in his stomach was not a good match for the blueberry muffin.

Shanny shifted her weight on the padded booth cushion and gently pushed the muffin aside. She cupped the tea with both hands. It was still steaming and had fogged her glasses, which she hadn't worn at the studio. She must have had her contacts on then.

"I just kept saying 'hey, I don't know, women can be funny' just to get him to calm down because he was getting a little agitated. Then a cab cut him off and he cursed and slammed on his horn. I didn't need any trouble."

It sounded like a very uncomfortable situation. Bo wondered if there was more.

"He seemed okay with changing the subject, but now he was focusing on me. He said I had a great voice and a hot body to go with it. At that point I pulled my jacket tighter around me and asked him politely to let me out."

"Oh my God. What an ass, to come on to you like that."

"Exactly. Anyway, here's the worst of it, he put his hand on my fucking leg. I was wearing that flowy, long skirt and had bunched it together in the middle so it was more comfortable in the car ride, and my legs were a little exposed. He felt it was perfectly fine to run his hand up my leg."

"Shit." Bo thought about how little Joey had changed since their younger days. "Sounds like he held you hostage."

"I would say so. I slapped his hand away and called him some choice words and started fidgeting with the door. I told him he'd better let me out or I was going to call the cops. There was a cop car near us in traffic and I was about to open the window and yell out to them or anybody who would listen."

"Oh my God. What did he do?" *Crazy-ass Joey.*

"He pulled over in a huff and said, 'Don't come looking for any more vocal work with us, bitch.' I pushed the door open and ran in the opposite direction so he couldn't follow me. We were on the West Side Highway near the midtown piers. There were lots of people out and lots of cars so he had to keep going."

"I can't believe I'm hearing this. And what he called you, so unbelievably disrespectful. What can I do to make things right?"

Bo was nervous for her response. He was already calculating what he'd have to do to take Joey off the project. Such talent, such a waste. What a despicable human being. *I should have known better than to get back in touch with him.*

"Really, there's nothing *to* do," Shanny said. "I know how much this means to you. Stef told me about your great-great uncle and his music. I just wish there were some way not to have my name associated with Joey."

It wasn't unreasonable. She wasn't even asking Bo to kick him off the CD, she just didn't want their names together. She understood that studio time was very expensive, and that they had made a really solid song together.

"I'll get another drummer if it's that important to you," said Bo. They could use the tracks from his bass and Shanny's vocals and the sound engineer could do some presto chango to splice in a new drummer. He was already thinking of who could sub. Jesse at the Minor Seventh knew some good drummers looking for work.

"Thank you but that's not necessary. How about not having my name or photo anywhere near his in the liner notes or in press photos or on social media, so I'm as far apart from him as humanly possible. And I won't do any interviews with him. Can we agree on that?"

"Easily done," said Bo, who meant it. "Again, I am so sorry. I had no idea that happened, and Stef did me a favor to tell me as soon as he did before you totally backed out of this. You're an amazing contributor to the CD and I'm so grateful you're staying on the project."

Shanny looked at him with tears in her eyes. This had shaken her. "I just got over a bad breakup. You know, Stef and I were something way back when. But since then it's been one bad relationship after another."

The last thing Bo was going to do was to put his hand on hers to comfort her. He just wanted her to be all right. "I'm sorry to hear that. Guys are not all pigs. But a lot of them are. You'll find the right one."

"I know." Shanny smiled. She looked very vulnerable. He knew how Stef had fallen for her. Why they broke up was another matter.

"I don't know how I'll bring this up to him, but he has to know his behavior is absolutely not acceptable. It's sexual battery any way you look at it. We don't want this kind of problem with our music so I'll need to speak to the other guys and see what we're going to do about it."

"I appreciate that," Shanny said. "I hope you don't mind me telling Stef. I was so upset that I wanted to quit working with male musicians altogether. I know that's not the right reaction."

"There's no wrong reaction. So don't worry about that. I'd probably feel the same way."

Shanny sipped the last of her tea until the tiny dregs were visible at the bottom of the cup. "They make the best muffins anywhere in the city. I'll vouch." She smiled.

"Me too."

"Well. Thanks again for hearing me out," she said. "I don't want to paint you all with the same brush. One bad apple. One bad drummer. You know."

Bo laughed. "Let me know if you need anything else. We're working on the artwork for the cover and like you mentioned, the liner notes. You and Joey will be very much separated. Also, can you send me a short bio and hi-res headshot?"

She nodded.

"One last and very important thing," he said.

"What's that?" Shanny felt she could trust him and was starting to feel better.

"On the CD itself, should we have Shanny or Chanel?"

"Chanel, please, no last name. That's how I go professionally."

"Done deal. I'm going to pay for our muffins up front. You're staying?" he asked.

"Nope. I've got things to do today. New music came in from my producer. We're doing a world jazz festival in the park next year and I have to learn the songs."

"Nice. Let's talk soon, okay?"

As he left the diner, he felt he had injected some sanity into a crazy situation. Working out the finer points of the CD cover and marketing materials so that Shanny would be happy was not an issue. As far as dealing with Joey, a decision was needed about keeping him or cutting him. Pip and Tim would have to weigh in.

CHAPTER 69

"Beyond the Bridge" had just been mastered and the track was ready to be placed onto the CD. It was an impeccable brew of sad and sultry vocals, cool vibrato on sax, silvery threads of counterpoint on piano and full satisfaction from the bass thanks to the brilliant Stef Dalton. Joey shimmered on drums. The song was everything Bo had wished for.

That was why he was so angry at Joey. This CD was going to be a stunner, every song a gem.

"I hate to mess with this," Bo said to Tim the next day, after recounting what Joey did. They were doing a video chat on Facebook.

Tim had just been meditating. He was so relaxed, it seemed like he was stoned, but he never touched drugs. He was just able to block out stress by letting go and breathing correctly.

"Listen, if you feel like you want to pull him, go ahead," Tim said. "There's definitely something broken about him, but I don't have a pony in this race. It's just that it will cost us more dough."

"For sure," said Bo. He was still agonizing over what Shanny told him and he had yet to approach Pip to see what he thought.

"You said Shanny seemed okay with keeping Joey in? I mean, you didn't think she would sue us or anything, do you?" Tim asked.

Bo was buttering an everything bagel to share with Margret. She was steeping Morning Sunrise tea, a blend of cherry and peppermint. "Maybe add in a sprinkle of fresh cocoa with that, hmmm?" he whispered to her.

"I don't think there are going to be any repercussions," Bo said to Tim. "Stef texted me last night, after Shanny and I met at the diner. He told me that Shanny felt a lot better about things."

"It's up to you and Pip, then. I'm neutral. The track is a beaut. You wrote a pretty ditty. They all are. Just see what Pip says and let me know."

"I already told him but he couldn't talk, something about having a date. I'll try him in a little while," Bo said. "The thing that gets me is that I wonder if Joey even knows how much he upset her, and all of us, with his crap."

"Who knows, man." Tim was thinking about starting his day. He was in the middle of Miles Davis's autobiography and was going to sit in his favorite chair facing the bay window that overlooked a neighborhood park.

"Oh, and I meant to tell you," said Bo. "I reached out to a graphic designer about the CD cover. I'm waiting to hear back."

"Cool!"

"But we have to decide pretty soon to be able to move ahead on this," said Bo. "About Joey. In or out?"

"It's all you, bro. Whatever you want to do. I guess Pip holds the answer, huh?"

Bo chewed his bagel. Margret hated when he made noise when he was eating. She shook her head at him.

"Timbo, I have a bagel to attend to and I'm getting the evil eye from the wife. Talk to you later. Enjoy Miles."

Bo waited until the afternoon to reach out to Pip. He had yet to relay the details of what happened with Joey. If Pip took a stand, there would be bigger things to worry about. Firing Joey, yes; but also remixing the song that had come out so perfectly. Lightning hardly ever strikes twice.

CHAPTER 70

Pip pedaled his bike harder to catch up with his new girlfriend Elisa. They were on the Hudson River Greenway and it was already the best date he'd ever had. His guest conducting gig in New York had turned into a temporary position and he was seriously considering leaving Boston for good.

He turned left to see the sun sparkling off the river, and for a moment, the air smelled fresh and autumnal. Then his phone buzzed. It was Bo.

"Hey hon, mind if I take this? It's CD stuff." She nodded and they gently swerved over to a bench along the path. They were almost at the top of the trail, under the George Washington Bridge which had a little lighthouse nearby. Elisa was a photographer and loved to capture New York City and its hidden surprises.

"Hey Bo, what's up? Sorry I sound out of breath, and yes, I'm being smart. I have my rescue inhaler with me. Elisa has me biking up the West Side."

"Well at least one of us is doing something healthy," said Bo. "Sorry to bother you on your date."

"It's fine. Everything okay?"

"I just wanted to take your temp on the thing with Joey. I started to tell you about it. Can you spare a couple of minutes?"

Pip wiped his forehead with a yellow bandana. "Lay it on me." His gaze drifted to Elisa, who was crouched down to get a good shot of the bridge. *Her jeans fit her nicely,* he thought.

"I met Shanny at a coffee shop for some damage control. Thank God she's okay with the CD, she just doesn't want her name or photo near Joey's on anything, like the CD or on social media."

"Understandable." Pip took a swig from his water bottle. It tasted warm and metallic. He looked for vendors selling water or Italian ices and didn't see any. "He's a real piece of work. But the CD came out so sweet, and mixing in my part and Tim's was immaculate. I don't know if we can replicate that magic with another percussionist or if we even have the time to find one. I vote to keep him in, mostly because Shanny is okay with it."

Bo relaxed into his club chair. "I was on the fence about it. I guess I have to agree with you. The greater good is that the CD is being made and it gives a voice to Lymus. One thing, though, I'm definitely having a talk with that boy. He has to know what he did was messed up."

"Agreed," said Pip. "I back that up one hundred percent. Anything else?"

"Sorry, I'm destroying your date. Something quick. I'm planning out the images for the CD cover. A photo shoot obviously isn't going to happen, not on our short deadline," said Bo. "My pic will be on the back. You know, the full-length shot of me that I use on everything."

"Good one. Love your old 'fro."

"Thanks. Me too. The hospital doesn't like when I wear it natural but I think I'm gonna start. Ha!" He was really going to think about it. Margret said he looked sexy with his hair free.

Bo continued. "The cover idea is sunlight coming through the trees. Six candles are in the foreground, five lit and one last one has the match about an inch away, ready to light it."

"I like it. Six for the six of us, including Stef and Shanny?"

"Right. But also, six for each decade Lymus was alive, which was something you couldn't have known. I think it's meaningful."

"Cool. Show us after you get some samples from the designer."

Bo loved how easy it was to talk to Pip. He wished he had seen more of his friend through the years, but then again, he could remedy that right now, starting today.

"You gonna bike already?" Bo asked.

"Yeah, if someone would stop holding me up. It's a beautiful day in Manhattan."

Thank God. Pip was the last holdout. They wouldn't have to re-record the CD. Now all that was left to do personnel-wise was reach out to Joey and get his bio and a few photos. The more serious discussion would have to wait.

CHAPTER 71

It was turning out to be a massively productive Thursday. Bo crossed a lot of items off his list and things were really starting to gel. He was praying for a quiet day in the ER so he could read and respond to all the emails going back and forth about production.

Bo had forwarded all the photos to Talia, who shortly came back to him with her mock-ups for the CD cover. They were amazing. She listened to Bo's ideas and designed a light blue and purple illustration with six lit candles providing a pop of neon yellow. A row of stylized southern magnolia trees stood tall in the background with the sun peeking through them. For the title, she used a wide, elegant font. The back cover had photos of the musicians, and she'd followed his explicit instructions to place Shanny at the far left and Joey at the far right. Talia reminded Bo to get a barcode, which he got quickly even though he hated putting his credit card information into his work computer. The barcode came back in an hour, which he immediately forwarded to Talia.

All six songs had miraculously been completed and were now at the mastering house. The engineer promised they'd be ready within the next seven days.

With the unmastered songs already in hand, Odessa was able to write her album review and add the list of songs and the musicians' bios. Bo was ecstatic with the results. Even though she was a classical music buff, she'd done her homework and learned the jazz vocabulary, giving each song an excellent description. Bo shared the writeup with the guys and with Shanny, who adored it and especially enjoyed being called "an intelligent siren with incredible poise and deft phrasing."

Then there was the merch. Bo paid Talia for the full rights to use the artwork and printed T-shirts, mugs and keychains.

The ER was its usual conglomeration of accidents, injuries, drunken stupors and cardiac issues. Bo couldn't wait to get home.

The door swung open. In walked Aimee. She had a problem.

CHAPTER 72

Aimee and Matt had just had an argument on the phone while she was on break. Now she was in a terrible mood. There was nothing left to do but dump on somebody else.

"Bo, I need to talk to you. It's not what you think."

Bo dreaded those words from anybody, especially Aimee, and especially now.

"What's going on?" He hated asking her an open-ended question.

"I know you're not a marriage expert or anything..."

What was that supposed to mean?

"Well, no, not at all. But what's the problem?" He looked over to the screen. All the rooms were clicked on. Maybe one of the reps would finish quickly and come into the office, a welcome disturbance to this conversation.

"It's Matt."

Oh. Thank God. I think.

"He doesn't want to come to the release party. He says he doesn't trust you."

Bo prayed for inner strength. "There's nothing I can do to help. I'm sorry he feels that way. If you like, I can send you the link when the show is put up online, or you can bring another friend."

"You don't seem to care," she said. She took a few steps closer and glared at him. For a moment he thought she was going to slap him. He couldn't think of what to do next.

He knew he'd have to talk to HR as soon as possible about her. He should have already done it.

On the screen, two new rooms turned red. "Looks like traumas. I'll help out," he said, as he headed towards the door. He didn't look back.

Somehow, she'd get him to care more. If he thought this wasn't a convenient time to talk, she'd find another time and the stakes would be much higher.

CHAPTER 73

More details sewn up.

Jesse confirmed the CD launch date with Bo: the second Friday in April at 8 p.m. His wife was still undergoing chemo, he said, and the good news was she was nearing the end of her treatments. He assured Bo that even if they had an emergency and had to go up to Westchester to see her specialist, his partner Tommy could run the club. "He's like the brother I never had," Jesse explained. "If he's running the show, you're in good hands. But I don't expect that to happen."

Now that the date was set in stone, Bo had to get moving with a social media marketing campaign. Margret was a whiz on Twitter and Instagram. She took over his @BoAbbottBass accounts and did her thing.

Tim McKnight dabbled in graphics so he took charge of designing flyers. Everyone pitched in to hang the flyers throughout their neighborhoods, even Stef, who knew a lot of club owners and musicians all over the tristate area. As for media outreach, Bo negotiated another $200 for Odessa to put together a media list and send out press releases. Pip helped Bo set up his Spotify, Bandcamp, Apple and Amazon accounts to sell the songs, and Joey sent Bo his formatted royalty spreadsheet.

The CD was a huge undertaking with a lot of moving parts. *Am I forgetting anything?* Bo wondered.

Just then an email came through from the mastering house. They couldn't complete "Beyond the Bridge" because copyright information was missing. "Failure to respond within 24 hours will forfeit our agreed-upon schedule and affect final production."

CHAPTER 74

Bo called the mastering house and asked for his account executive, James Ivey. "Mr. Ivey isn't here at the moment," said the receptionist. "He's out with a client. We expect him back in about an hour." It was already 3 p.m. Even if they stayed open until 5, it didn't necessarily mean Ivey would be back from his meeting.

"Okay. Can you please give him a message to call me? This is Bo Abbott and I'm responding to his email about a copyright issue."

"Sure can. Thank you, sir."

Their twenty-four-hour deadline still meant that the next morning would be fine – unless they were closed on Fridays.

Bo's nerves were jangled.

In the meantime, he decided to be proactive, calling Stef to try to sort this out. It went immediately to voice mail. "Hey Stef! It's Bo. The mastering guy needs copyright info on our song together. Please call me as soon as you can. Thanks."

He didn't want to pressure Stef but if the issue wasn't resolved soon, it could jeopardize the timing of the CD.

At 4:30, Bo called Ivey again and was met with the same answer: he was still out. When Bo asked for his cell, the receptionist said he couldn't provide it.

At 5, Bo was almost frantic. He knew he had the whole next morning, but there was no telling how busy the ER would be, and with Aimee apparently on edge and sporting a newfound desire to harass him, it would be even harder to resolve this from work.

When he was ready to go home the clock read 6:10 p.m. Second shift was now humming and doing its own thing. All was well. His phone started humming too. It was a text from Stef.

Hey Bo got yr msg. All is perfection. You own the copyright and I'm only a guest. What do I need to sign? It's usu just standard paperwork. Let me know.

That was a relief. It sounded like Stef had come across this before and that it wasn't that big a deal.

He said goodbye to his second shifters, hopped on and then off the subway and ran up the steps to the street level. When he got home, he pushed the door open with such force that it almost knocked over Margret, who was on her way to the dumbwaiter with a bag of garbage. "Hold on!" she snapped.

"Sorry honey! The mastering house needs some documentation that could hold up everything. I have 24 hours or they can delay the last song."

Margret deposited the bag into the slot and went back over to Bo. "Hugs first. Now, what about the CD?"

"Okay, so all songs have copyrights, and as you know, all the material on the CD is original. I own the copyright."

"Come on in the house."

Bo realized he sounded like a crazy man.

"Why are you so excited?" she asked.

"The mastering exec emailed me."

"And?"

"My head's going to explode. The email said there's missing documentation for the song with Stef. I guess Ivey guy knows of Stef and he – Ivey – wants to know who owns the rights to the song Stef plays on. By the time I called his office, I had missed him. I have to get this done ASAP."

Margret was starving. She'd gotten in only a few minutes before Bo and was trying to put something together for dinner. Pasta and meat sauce with sliced veggies was just about the quickest thing to do unless they'd spring for take-out.

It was a messed-up day at work for her. Dennis was acting like an idiot again with a female co-worker, and her boss was questioning her about the font on their mammogram brochures. St. Cecil's was as maddening as New York County General.

"Why not just call them tomorrow?" she asked, stifling her impatience.

"I plan to. But they said if I didn't have this issue sewn up within 24 hours, it would delay the project. I have so much riding on it." Bo put his head in his hands. Already the onions and peppers were starting to smell amazing and he realized how hungry he was.

"Did you reach out to Stef?"

"Yeah, and he texted me right back. He said there should be standard paperwork and he'd sign off on it."

Bo took a pull from a chilly bottle of Michelob and texted Stef again. *Sorry to bother you. The master house is closed for the day and the guy didn't send me any paperwork. It has to be resolved by tomorrow before noon or it will stall the project indefinitely. I will update you then, thanks.*

It could be a waiting game. He hated to cause Stef any reason to worry, but he had to get his signature on whatever document they needed.

Just before 11 p.m. when he and Margret were about to call it a night, a text came in from Stef.

No issues here. Call them in the am and forward the doc to me. I'll sign it right quick. Peace out.

It was not a restful evening for Bo. Margret had the benefit of a few sips of Merlot and was already out. He heard her snoring and put his earplugs in.

This is modern romance, he thought.

CHAPTER 75

Lymus and Callista – who could only ever be together in the abstract world of words and ideas, not physical reality – had only encountered one another on rare occasions, and that was in the prep kitchen. She was 15 at the time, Lymus was 18. She'd dotter down the uneven stairs to enter a room filled with steam. She often lingered on the last step to take in the wonderful aromas and say a silent prayer to God thanking Him for her life, bounty and freedom, while asking Him to make the house slaves free to live on their own and raise their own families.

Her task was to inspect the potatoes. For almost a year, she would drag out her responsibilities and spend as much time as possible in the prep kitchen without bringing attention to herself. Slowly she wound through the crowded room to the vegetable cook, passing Lymus on the way and gifting him with a furtive smile. His heart leaped out of his tattered shirt. When he was feeling particularly bold, he'd meet Callista's eyes and smile back. The chemistry between the two was unmistakable, and in another place and time, they could openly allow their mutual admiration to develop.

Lymus's dream was tragically cut short about a year later when Callista was thrown from a horse and sustained a head injury. She died at the tender age of 16.

Lymus composed one last song in her honor, but lacked the energy to notate it. It died with him decades later when his own life ended, still enslaved, at the age of 60 due to heart failure, a medical condition as well as an emotional state.

Bo could not have known this much about Lymus's life but he knew the approximate dates that bookmarked his existence. He wanted the CD to be a celebration of that life, a span of six decades filled with hope and love and music.

CHAPTER 76

Joey hadn't heard anything about the CD for over a week. Last he spoke to Bo, the masters were being finalized. He couldn't wait to hear the tracks all clean and edited.

What happened with Shanny was a bummer, but it was her loss, no skin off his nose, as they say. Joey knew he was irresistible. Plenty of women told him that. It was his blue eyes and dark lashes, and the fact that he could kill the shit out of any rhythm.

He thought of calling Shanny to see if she was still pissed off. That was a weird afternoon, to say the least. Here she was, this truly beautiful and talented lady, who smiled at him as if to say she wanted to get to know him better. He knew the cues. *Maybe I moved too fast?*

He picked up his phone and at the last second decided to call Bo instead. There had been no word on a launch date at The Minor Seventh.

Bo picked up on the first ring. He wanted to get this over with.

"Hey Joey, what's going on?" Bo tried to sound friendly but it wasn't translating.

"Just stuff and things, my friend. Hey, I wanted to find out about the release party and all. What's the latest?"

Bo wasn't up to an electronic intervention and resolved to avoid the topic of Shanny. He'd keep this fast and light.

"Good things all around," said Bo. "The tracks are being completed by the mastering house and they should be up on Soundcloud soon. I'll send you a link. We got a date, April ninth at eight."

"Fantastic! We're good, then?" Joey asked.

Bo fell silent as he tried to figure out what to say next. He could hear Joey blowing out cigarette smoke.

"I think that's it!" Bo tried to squeeze some cheer into his voice.

Joey cleared his throat.

"So Bo. I have to ask you something."

"What, man?"

"Did Shanny say anything to you about me?"

There it is.

All kinds of responses flooded Bo's frontal cortex. He chose the most noncommittal. "Yeah, kinda. She said you made a pass at her but she wasn't interested. She talked more about the music, and wanted to know if she sounded raspy. She'd just gotten over a cold."

"Yeah, it was a whole lot of nothing. Anyway, I think she sounded great."

More silence followed.

"Hey Joey."

"What?"

"There's something I want to add." *This needs to be said.* "Shanny was extremely upset about you driving her home. According to her, you were completely out of place. I mean, touching her leg? Come on, man!"

"That's chicks for you. Over-sensitive. She didn't want to smash together, no big deal."

Of course he'd be a dick about it.

"Look," said Bo. "I wasn't there, but from what she said, you might be facing lawsuits in your future if you don't cut this out. Whatever went down, I don't want anybody victimized on my watch. Just letting you know so you stay far away from her. And don't talk to her at all on release day. I'm not fucking kidding."

Joey nearly dropped his phone. "Hey, no need to be so heavy. I'll leave her be."

Did Bo get his point across?

Joey spoke next. "Okay, well, thanks for the update."

Big checkmark on Bo's list. He had no idea the process was going to be so emotionally draining.

Now if he could just confirm the copyright issue and get the masters done, things could move forward.

CHAPTER 77

It was 9 a.m. on Friday. Bo called James Ivey. *I have so much riding on every cog turning smoothly,* he thought. *I hope this Ivey guy doesn't give me a hard time.*

"Stellar Sonic, how can I help." The bored voice didn't even care enough to add the upwards inflection that formed a question.

"James Ivey please, this is Bo Abbott, and it's urgent."

"One moment."

The line rang five times. On the sixth, he picked up. "Ivey. Yes." Another non-question.

"This is Bo Abbott, returning your call." Bo's heart was pumping a dance in his temples.

"Oh yes, hi. We had some issues with the song 'Beyond the Bridge' in that we were lacking approval from a Mr. Stefanie – sorry, Stefan Dalton."

Bo felt his hands go clammy. "Yes. I spoke to him and he said he would sign off on the rights affirmation and fax it back to you as soon as possible. Can you please send that to me?"

Ivey took his time. "I would do that right now, but I'm in the middle of an issue with another client." Big surprise. "Give me an hour or so."

"Okay but Mr. Ivey, you said we have until noon."

"I'm aware." There was a hint of sarcasm in his response. "I will get it to you before 10 a.m. Mark my words."

All the rooms in the ER were full. Aimee was out for a doctor's visit. Just then, he remembered he wanted to go to HR and tell them about what was going on with her.

One of the registration reps, Carol, came into the office. She was a breath of fresh air. Mature, responsible and pleasant as the day is long.

"Hi Carol. Can you do me a favor?"

"Sure thing, Bo, what is it?" She had wheeled in her COW and was watching the screen.

"You're all okay out there? I see all the patients have been registered. We're at max capacity."

"No room at the inn, as they say," she quipped. "What do you need?"

"I need to go to HR and file some medical paperwork. Mind the store for a few?"

"No problem. I just wanted to take a few minutes to get off my feet, since we're all caught up at the moment."

"Sit, please. Thanks for keeping an eye out. I'll be back soon."

No email from Ivey yet. The time waiting and worrying would be better spent taking care of another to-do item.

And away we go.

The conversation went surprisingly well. The HR director was very sympathetic and asked him to document what he'd told her in writing. "I'm glad you talked to me. When you write it up, we'll put it in your personnel file," she said. "As far as writing up your staff member, Aimee Patel, her evaluation comes up at the end of April, about a month away. Hopefully she calms down and there are no further incidents."

It was the first piece of good news he'd received in a while. He didn't have to deal with the issue right now, unless she did anything new that was inappropriate or insubordinate.

The meeting with HR took forty minutes. Bo went into the atrium for a breather. There was a Starbucks kiosk in the lobby. Fate was favoring him.

He felt his phone vibrate in his pocket. It was an email from Ivey, who'd sent the necessary affirmation form. Bo thanked him and forwarded the email to Stef. He hoped Stef was near a computer to sign it and then return it to Bo. Things were turning around.

The coffee tasted burnt, but this was what he liked about it. He took it black. Deep, mellow and potent.

The level of activity in the atrium was amazing. County General never stopped, never slowed. Bo allowed it to sink in and watched from a detached perspective.

Not a bad place to work, he thought. He missed Margret during the day, though. They used to have lunch together a few times a week.

His reverie was interrupted with another email. Stef had signed the document. Bo forwarded it to Ivey and dialed him up.

"James Ivey, please." *Don't tell me he's busy.*

"Ivey. What?"

"Hi Mr. Ivey, this is Bo. Stef Dalton signed the form. I just emailed it to you. Please tell me if you received it?"

The next moment took too long to come.

"Let me check. One minute."

In the ensuing silence, Bo thought about his timeline and the delicate dance of scheduling all the marketing around the April ninth release at The Minor Seventh. On Odessa's instructions he had invited the local press, a few muckity-mucks from the Rutgers University Jazz Program, and the coordinators of the annual jazz festival 75 miles away in a town called Delaware Water Gap in Pennsylvania.

Ivey got back on the line. His voice was bland. "I have it. Good thing you called. We're slammed here, and given a few more hours, I would've had to put you further back in the schedule."

Even split four ways, Bo and the other guys paid a pretty penny to get the mastering completed on time. Thank God there would be no delays.

"Then we're good?" Bo asked.

"Right as rain."

It was time to check in with Jesse and make sure he had everything he needed. As a club owner, he'd have some influence to bring in a few jazz VIPs for the big event. What could possibly go wrong?

CHAPTER 78

The countdown had officially started: two weeks out to the release party.

And like a bolt out of the blue he realized what was missing: a video for YouTube, just a teaser, that would spread the word on the upcoming release date and let people know about the CD itself. There wasn't a lot of time left, but he had to make the effort.

He reached out to Odessa. She'd done such a great job on the liner notes. Maybe she knew a videographer. He'd take anyone at this point.

"You're in luck," Odessa told him. "I know a video guy. Whether he's free or not is another thing. His name is Leo and he runs a company called The Glaring Lion. I guess that's an inside joke."

Bo smiled. Hopefully this lion was fast.

"It's worth a shot. At this late date I don't have a lot of choice in the matter. Can I tell him you sent me?"

"Definitely. We refer each other all the time. He does great work, by the way."

Time was not on Bo's side. Leo was working through lunch and took the call. He was excited to hear about the new album with Stef Dalton, and then told Bo that because he was a friend of Odessa's, he'd knock 10% off his first-timer's price.

"You didn't give yourself a lot of time," Leo said. "Or me. I'm going to have to work super hard to fit this in."

"I know. That's my bad. It's my first rodeo. We didn't even know if this CD was going to be a thing until this morning."

"I'll do my best. Can you get the musicians all together in one place before next week?"

Bo's heart sank. "Not really. Two are out of town, and you know Stef, well, I hate to take up his time because he has so many other projects on the front burner, and Shanny, or rather Chanel, is building her career..."

"She sure is. What a powerhouse! You were lucky to grab her for this album."

"Don't I know it," said Bo. "Is there any way we can still try?"

"Maybe. You said you recorded some of it at the studio?"

"I did, but it was just myself, my drummer and Shanny on my iPhone." Bo realized Shanny didn't want to be anywhere near Joey. "The footage is not bad. One stipulation though. This is confidential."

"Tell me."

"The drummer and Shanny don't get along. Seriously. So you need to keep them in different frames. Is that doable?"

"I need to see what you have," said Leo. "How about stills of you all? I have plenty of stock instrument photos I can use but I might not even have to."

Bo perked up. "We have a lot of stills. There are a few photos of us from years ago when we played in college and I have the headshots that everybody turned in for the CD cover."

"We can definitely do something with all that. Do you have any of the masters? I'd like to get maybe two songs and we'll play bits and pieces. You'll see. I think you'll be surprised at what we come up with."

"Then you don't need me in the studio?" he asked.

"No. Long as you don't mind, I'll do the voiceover for it. I've been doing a lot of that. Send me your bios and a short writeup on the music. If you have a press release, send that too. I'll do some sleight of hand. Don't worry, it'll come together."

Bo had no doubt about that. But the timing was another thing. "I hate to ask, but – when might the video be done?"

Leo looked up at his whiteboard and grimaced. Luckily Bo couldn't see that. "You said the release is on April ninth, so I can get this to you by the first. That gives you a week to have everybody make this go viral. But just to let you know, this is going to be super short, like under three minutes," he said. "We could expand on that in the future. Will that work for you?"

"Absolutely. Any advice on making it go viral?"

"Yeah," said Leo. "Work that media list Odessa put together for you. Those are the exact people who need to see this video. And then, run like hell and tell everybody to be ready to blast it all over social media, every day, until the release."

Bo took a moment to think about his next steps.

"Why are you still there? I've got a video to do."

CHAPTER 79

Friday, 5:30 a.m. Bo's inbox pinged with a video attachment. It was from Leo.

"Mags, when you get out of the shower, come over because – GUESS WHAT?"

"Yeah?" She'd just stepped out, squeezing the towel over her wet hair. Her jeans and a white blouse were lain out on the bed for Casual Friday.

Bo hopped into a leg of his pants while trying to play the video on his phone.

"Is that from Leo?"

"It is."

"You actually waited for me?" Margret was amazed.

"Almost didn't, but yes."

The video started playing. Margret recognized the theme of "Beyond the Bridge" and she batted away her tears. Bo was shocked in place, his jaw slack. "This is unreal," he mumbled.

Leo's editing was tight and sharp. Photos of the band members faded in and out, and the voiceover was rich, almost sultry. Right before the three-minute mark, a shot of the CD cover appeared and then blurred, replaced by the words "RELEASE DATE: APRIL 9" and the band's Facebook page.

"Bo, your mouth is open," Margret said.

"Wow. Is that high production value or what? Leo's like a wizard or something."

She nodded. "You pulled this together pretty fast. When are you going to post this? Can you get some time at lunch to make it happen?"

"I have to," he said. "I told you I'm under strict orders to blast this to outer space. Maybe I'll even send one to Fetterman. What the hey."

Bo thought he was being thorough, but of all the things he did to make the CD become a reality, that last one would turn out to be the most dangerous.

CHAPTER 80

Bo scribbled his index finger on the UPS signature pad and nodded to the driver, who handed over the envelope.

The return address showed a post office box from Scarsdale, NY. It wasn't his birthday and he wasn't late on any bills. This was something mysterious to ponder.

Bo sat at the kitchen table and pulled the tab on the back of the envelope. As his eyes began to scan the letter inside, he turned to stone. He could not believe what he saw.

Margret came into the kitchen to make a kale smoothie, preparing for some light mockery from Bo, when she saw him put his head on the table. The only other time she'd seen him like that was when he got his rejection for mentoring at Jazz at Lincoln Center. He never quite gotten over it, but he found out later that the program was overstaffed, so it wasn't a slight on him personally.

"What's wrong, sweetie?"

Bo rubbed his eyes. "That asshat is suing me."

Anybody could sue anyone for anything, something she knew all too well from hearing about frivolous malpractice lawsuits at the hospital. It didn't mean any of them had merit or that anyone would ever see the inside of a courtroom. "What is he suing for? I can't possibly imagine...?" she asked.

The letterhead looked menacing. It was the top entertainment law firm from Albany, New York, with a three-word admonishment that sent Bo's blood pressure through the roof. "CEASE AND DESIST" it read.

Apparently, Bernard Fetterman was of the belief that the third song on his CD, and therefore the entirety of the CD since the songs were "intellectually inseparable," plagiarized the hit song from *The Scandals of Violet*. He demanded the CD be pulled or intimated that Bo was risking a quick and costly litigation.

"How could he possibly know this?" Margret demanded. "You didn't even have your release date yet!"

"I sent him the link to the video we did."

"Oh no."

"It doesn't matter. This music is going to be out in a week. This sure is some David versus Goliath bullshit!" Bo growled. "He ripped off Lymus, and if there's one thing I know about human nature, it's that he knows it. Or at least he knew it in 1935. That's why he feels so threatened."

Margret thought of something even scarier, and as soon as the shadow crossed her face, her husband sat bolt upright. "What is it?" he asked her.

"Turn to the second page. I just want to see if there's anything else in the letter."

Sure enough, right after the over-confident, loopy signature reading "Bernard Jerome Fetterman" was a cc for Stef Dalton.

CHAPTER 81

Bo was in a panic.

Zack had dealt with cease-and-desist letters many times before and tried to get Bo to calm down. "C&Ds are designed to get the recipient to freak out," he told Bo. "It's usually just somebody flexing their muscles and nothing more."

"I hope you're right, man. When Stef gets his copy of the letter, though, he's going to regret he ever got into this project." The cat was out of the bag. The music was on every platform and in less than a week had write-ups in blogs and online publications. Everybody wanted to know how they got Stef Dalton on board.

"Let's not jump to conclusions," Zack said. "Have you talked to Stef, to brief him this?" He was thinking four steps ahead and wasn't overly alarmed. Just as Bo couldn't pinpoint with certainty the provenance of the music from the Civil War Museum, neither could Bernard Fetterman turn around and prove that Bo had stolen the music from *him*.

"I called Stef right away. He understood and said he'd let me handle it, unless I needed his input. He's a real mensch. This is just so embarrassing for me." Bo had let his coffee go cold, and the New York Times, part of his Sunday ritual, was now a scuffle of broadsheets on the couch. He had been scanning the arts section for some mention of his CD. No press coverage from the Old Gray Lady yet.

"Listen. We can't absolutely prove the music came from your great-great uncle, and Fetterman's lawyer can't prove where your music came from either. I assume your computer files are dated, showing when you started writing the song?"

Bo hadn't thought of that. "Yes. It was before the play debuted on Broadway. It was even before Fetterman's new music was registered with ASCAP. I checked."

"Almost a lawyer yourself. That's my pal."

"Zack, you understand that no matter what can or can't be proven, he can still exert pressure on me to nix the song, right?"

Zack hated how the filthy rich thought they were exempt from the code of human decency. "He can try anything, but it doesn't mean it'd be within his rights to, and that you couldn't countersue."

"Not that I'd want to."

"No."

"Well, then. What now? Sit back and wait for the other shoe to drop?" Bo asked.

Zack also hated that the courts were clogged with meaningless, pissing-contest litigation. Yet, some of that was his bread and butter.

"Bo. Don't do anything. Forget about it for now. I'll make a call. I am ninety-nine percent sure that this is just a huge fuss about the old man losing his relevance. Go enjoy those big royalties on your streaming songs."

"Right on. Sixty-seven cents really gets my gears cranking. But okay. I'll do my best. Stay in touch and regards to the wife."

The next communique from the Fetterman camp would come from the son, Bruce, after release day, by which time Bo felt sure that it had blown over.

He was wrong.

CHAPTER 82

On the Wednesday before the big day, Bo planned to grab a downtown bus after work and drop in at the club. Jesse had been holding open mic on Wednesdays so Bo knew he'd be prepping in the kitchen and making sure the bar was stocked.

"Hey Jesse!"

He was slicing limes. "Hey Bo, how's the fiddle?"

"I just came by to see what's going on and ask if you needed any help for the big night." Bo noticed his friend's eyes were puffy.

Jesse sniffed and shook it off. "Nope. We're on track. I'm excited to see how this all comes together. How are you?"

"I'm pretty good, thanks. Had a little snafu with clearing the rights to one of the songs. They thought maybe Stef owned it. But that's resolved." He paused for a few beats. "Are you doing okay?"

Jesse put down the knife. "It's Kim. We had a setback."

"Oh no. I'm sorry to hear. What's going on?"

"They thought she had clear margins on the cancer, but they found a few more cells. That means another surgery. The good thing is, they said they were very sparse, and with the patterning they can do now, it's even more precise than when she was diagnosed."

It truly sucked to hear this. Bo felt terrible. He didn't want to bring up the release party, but he wanted to reassure Jesse that if the date had to be delayed, it was okay. Lots of things are more important than a CD.

"You shouldn't worry, though," Jesse said. "Tommy can run things incredibly smoothly. In fact, you won't even notice he's there. He'll let the kitchen and the bar do what they do, and he's such a people-person that he'll probably get more folks in the door."

"Thanks for saying that. I really do appreciate you."

Jesse walked over to the cash register and poked around for a business card. "Here's his info. It'd be a good idea for you to reach out to him, pre-emptively. He can spread the word to his contacts. He belongs to a super-huge Universal Unitarian church in Queens and they all love jazz. I shit you not."

It was good to see Jesse smile.

"Thanks, I'll definitely do that," Bo said. "Is Kim around? I'd like to thank her too, in advance."

Jesse released a dim smile. "Sorry, she's resting at home. But she gets out for a two-mile walk every few days and it keeps her strong and in a good frame of mind, which is where I need to be. All about cuttin' those limes. Hey, that's a good song title, isn't it?"

CHAPTER 83

All the plans that could have possibly been made, all the mapping out, the contingencies and the what-ifs had come to this. It was the night before the release party. A cool April evening in Brooklyn, starry and calm. At 3:30 a.m., Bo couldn't relax his brain.

"Can't sleep?" Margret had already gotten six hours of sleep. It would be enough. Bo was buzzing with adrenaline.

"Sorry, did I wake you up?" he asked.

"Not at all. Excited, huh?"

Bo turned on his side and put his arm over her body. Moonlight filtered in from the blinds and traced the contour of her face. "I don't know how I'm going to get through work today," he said. "I feel like we're missing something."

"This is just like pre-wedding jitters. You and the guys, you did everything possible to prepare for this. Now it's up to all the music lovers out there to show up." She shimmied closer and kissed him.

"Jesse, man, he did everything to make this possible, and with his wife sick...I just don't know what kind of guy does this."

"A friend. And giving half the door for their medical expenses is really sweet."

"I'm happy to give my whole take back to him. You okay with that?"

They were an ordinary American couple, living paycheck to paycheck in a city where rents were ridiculous. But they were comfortable enough, and they weren't struggling. Being paid for the gig was almost superfluous. Margret didn't mind if he gave back his portion. The potential benefit in exposure was worth it, to say nothing of the fact that Lymus's story would finally be told.

"I'm very okay with it. You are some kinda guy."

Unfortunately, somebody else thought the same thing of him and she wasn't about to disappear any time soon.

CHAPTER 84

Matt Singelli was getting a little annoyed that Aimee wouldn't stop talking about the show at a club called The Minor something. He didn't like jazz and he wasn't keen on meeting Aimee's supervisor. *He's probably a creeper who has the hots for her,* Matt thought. *He'll probably get the wrong idea when he sees her at his show tomorrow night.*

"Can we skip it?" he asked. They were in the living room watching a campy murder mystery. There was never anything good on cable. He kept changing channels and grunting about the news, which he wanted to avoid at all costs. The media from the left and the right were closing in on him and crushing his soul.

Aimee couldn't help herself. She put her hand on the remote. She wanted to fling it across the room. "Matt, I told you how important this is to me."

"And why is that? Hot for teacher?"

Aimee knew she was turning red, but the room was dimly lit so he couldn't read her face. She was letting a pan of ratatouille simmer on the stove and the aroma helped calm her down. She liked to use shallots, but she had to roast them separately because Matt hated anything oniony.

"Just stop," she said, composing herself. "I think a few other people from work are going to be there. And we never go out to do anything fun anymore." She'd need to fix that soon, set the tone, before they became husband and wife.

"Yeah, but jazz?" He was almost whining. It wasn't attractive. "You went out to that club before, didn't you? So now you're suddenly a jazz fan?"

These were the inane conversations that made Aimee take pause. Ten, twenty or thirty more years of this? Matt was adorable and cared about things like the environment, working out and taking care of himself. He was smart, funny and so handsome. Like, a knockout. But sometimes they weren't on the same page.

"I know," she persisted. "You let me drag you to the community theater my old friends are in, even though you don't really want to be there. But I'm just saying, it'll be a fun night out. That's all. Something different."

Matt got up to check on the pan and decided to add another splash of wine. He turned up the heat. "You like when the eggplant gets a little sticky and kind of burned, right?"

"Sure." She was trying not to get nasty.

"Listen, I'll go," he said. "I'll grade papers during my office hours in the morning. They're not expecting their grades back until Monday, anyway."

She softened. "Thanks. I knew you'd see it my way." She hugged him from behind and leaned her head into him. He smelled of Armani. She needed to update his cologne to something more contemporary. He was a little bit of a square, but marriage is all about compromises.

I can't wait to see Bo on the stage tomorrow. Maybe I can sneak a little somethin'-somethin' in for one last time. And after this, I'll definitely cool it.

CHAPTER 85

The extra houselights were on and Jesse was arranging the tables and chairs when Bo and Margret walked in.

"Bo!" Always a friendly reception from Jesse and always a bear hug to go with it. Margret grinned.

"Hey Jesse. I'm so psyched to be here! I thought three hours early gave us enough time." He felt out of breath. This was thrilling and terrifying all at once. "Did I miss anything? What do you need me to do?"

Margret looked around the room. Even more than packing the house or looking for journalists, she just wanted him to have a great time. It would be a memorable night no matter what. She just didn't realize how memorable.

"How's your wife? Is she here?" Bo said a quick and silent prayer for his and Margret's health and for Jesse's wife.

"Hanging on, staying strong. She's at home, baking. It makes her happy. I think she likes making me fat. And that's just fine with me."

Bo placed several boxes of CDs on the floor and set up a colorful table display he'd ordered online, along with a stand-up poster of the album cover. Time was ticking away. "I hope Stef and Shanny have reliable transportation," he said to nobody in particular. Then he remembered Joey and he prayed again; this time, that Joey wouldn't pull any crap and just be the kick-ass drummer he needed to be tonight.

Jesse pointed to the stage. "I'm going to leave everything to you and the guys, however you set things up. I did want to ask you about the announcements. It's really okay for me to mention the fundraiser?" Tears sprang to his eyes.

Margret went to hug him. "Of course," she said. "Without you, there's no debut, and this is not about the money for us, it's about exposure and getting this music heard." Bo cocked his head at her. She smiled. Money would be nice too.

Bo's phone was blowing up. Over the next half hour, each of the band members checked in; they were all on the way, the core guys and then Shanny who said she was sharing a ride downtown with Stef. Bo started breathing more normally until he remembered that he'd invited the entire ER staff...and the registration reps. There was no telling whether Aimee would come, and if she did, if she brought her plus-one. Time for one more prayer.

CHAPTER 86

Aimee sprayed a circle of scent around herself, a homemade concoction of tea tree oil with a lily base. She waved the air to disperse it and caught her reflection in the bathroom mirror. *I'm drawing in some fierce eyelash wings tonight,* she thought. *With a white tightline to brighten my eyes.* Matt loved it when she wore makeup when they went out. He told her she "sizzled" and he couldn't wait to get her home.

There would be no rushing out of anywhere tonight, though.

"It's nice that you support your supervisor. The makeup being hot is just a coincidence, huh?" Matt had come up behind her and placed his hands on her hips, pressing into her with increased pressure.

"Well, I'm a career-minded woman, so there's that." Aimee twisted around and looked up into Matt's eyes. After a warm, slow kiss, Matt pulled back. "Do we have time?"

He's trying to be respectful of my plans for tonight, but why doesn't he just take me? she wondered.

"Yes, we do," she purred, recognizing her own desire in the way her breath caught. And also, she realized, a little intimacy now would calm him down and keep him from being jealous at the club.

Just give me some breathing room tonight, she thought. *It's all I'm asking.*

CHAPTER 87

At 7:15 p.m. Joey came bounding into The Minor Seventh almost shoulder-to-shoulder with Shanny, only because Stef was a gentleman and had let her go ahead of him. He didn't see that Joey had squeezed his way in at the same time. The slitted eyes and tight-lipped expression on the old man's face said it all.

Joey had both arms filled with accessories for his drum kit. "Sorry, 'scuse me, sorry!" he said, almost making a scene. Shanny let him pass and gave Bo a look, but then she smiled and added a thumbs up.

Stef seemed a little annoyed at Joey's presence, but he was a pro and wouldn't let it affect the performance. Shanny sidled up to Stef and put her arm around his waist, giving him a secret little squeeze. It was her way of telling him to chill; Joey wasn't anybody worth worrying about. He wouldn't be a problem anyway, because of all the beautiful women who were about to fill the room.

Stef's grandson appeared, wheeling in Stef's famous bass (Monk had supposedly inscribed the back with his trademark upwards arrow symbol). Tim McKnight gave an effusive and affectionate greeting to Margret, and Pip Jones wrestled his way to the stage with his tenor still in its case.

A young woman with a press pass at the end of a lanyard stood in the doorway, asking for Bo. One of the waitresses pointed to the stage. "Big guy hauling that second bass over to the stage," she said. "That's Bo."

"Excuse me, Bo Abbott?" the woman asked.

He turned around. "That's me," he grinned.

"Hi, I'm Stacey Redbone, and I'm from USA Today."

Bo couldn't believe his ears. "Well, hello Stacey! Have you come to hear some amazing music?"

"Absolutely! I'll be able to stay for the first set only. Could you slip-slide out at the break for some quick questions?"

Bo was still in disbelief. Margret watched it unfold and understood this was media exposure they wouldn't dare to dream up. "For sure, just wave me out when you're ready," he stammered. Thank God he brought a few copies of his press kit. "Let me give you one of these so you have my background and pictures, and of course the CD. I'm so honored you came out to see us!" The clock was inching ahead and the set-up was far from complete.

"Sounds good. I'll come up to the stage then and maybe we can talk in the owner's office?"

Jesse, who had overheard, nodded his head violently. Bo almost burst out laughing.

"That'll work."

"Well, knock 'em out!" Stacey said, making her way to a small table off to one side.

A new silhouette appeared in the doorway, again female, this time with long, gleaming hair. Aimee's eyes searched the room and waved at Bo, who gave a short, unenthusiastic wave back. She started towards the stage, putting distance between her and the older man behind her. When Matt got close enough to her he whispered, "Do we have to be all the way up front?"

Aimee whipped around, abruptly changing her glaring expression to an aggressive smile. "Yes honey. We do."

The Minor Seventh was teeming with people happy to pay the small cover charge to hear Stef and whoever that other bassist was. *It's fine,* thought Bo. *I knew he'd be the draw, but this gets me seen and heard. Nothing wrong with that picture.*

Aimee noticed Stacey Redbone and couldn't place her, but then she saw the press pass dangling from the woman's neck. She scoped the room for Margret and found her talking with Bo, who was trying to tune his bass. He leaned down from the stage and they kissed, briefly, but it was long enough to make Aimee want to scream.

"What do you want to drink?" Matt asked her.

"A martini, straight up." She considered adding *make that two* but held herself in check.

Aimee didn't have a plan so much as an end goal, which was to get close enough to feel Bo's body heat – somehow – and finish what she had started at this very club months ago. She'd already applied for another registration position at the hospital's medical office and figured it was all for the best. Her last hurrah, though, wouldn't be denied.

CHAPTER 88

Bo stepped up to the microphone to do the intros. The crowd had been sufficiently warmed up from the first two songs and, judging from the enthusiastic cross-conversations, they were well-lubricated.

"Ladies and gents!" he said, peering around the room. "The lights, they're blinding! Ha! But I'm so happy you're here. Thanks for coming out. I mean, get this weather. April and still cold as hell. Y'all will be freezing your tushies off when you leave." Chuckles followed.

"This music is a journey, but I promise to give you the short version. See, I'd found out nearly a year ago that I have a great-great uncle who was a musician. And also a slave. My family believes that this brave and amazing soul, Lymus Jefferson Abbott, wrote a song that goes like this." Bo played a passage on his bass. "And it has seemed to me that this resembles the music from a very well-known opera in the early 1930s."

How far did he want to go with this? There was no reason to stir anything up and cause a chain reaction that could result in a lawsuit. He'd already endured a brush with the beginnings of one and avoiding legal troubles had become his primary objective in life.

"This has become my personal mission. My wife never got tired of hearing about it." Bo bowed his head to her, placing his hand on his heart. "My friends were intrigued. My family was supportive. But since there is no surefire way to prove its provenance, a fancy word I learned and love to use now, I had to do something else with all this energy. And hence we have 'Lines for Lymus'. A huge shout out for these amazing cats behind me who helped create this music. Joey Fritz on drums!" Joey took a mallet to the cymbals. "Pip Jones on sax! Tim McKnight on keys! And for the most amazing guest musicians ever, Chanel on vocals!" Bo knew he'd have to wait for the applause to subside. "And this icon of bassology, the inimitable Stef Dalton!" More applause and hoots of admiration followed.

"Thank you to Jesse and Kim for making this evening possible, grab a CD if you can, and enjoy the music!"

Bo turned around and reminded the musicians that Stef was going to take the stage, something they had worked out beforehand. They were going to follow him on a spirited cover of "Goody Goody" before continuing with the music from the CD.

Bo took off past the stage to the restrooms. When he came out, who was standing there, right near those stupid black and white photos?

Aimee.

CHAPTER 89

Queasiness grabbed him by the gonads, but Bo was resolute. This time, he wouldn't be stopping for chit-chat. "Hey," he said, whisking by her.

"Bo, wait!" she cried out. He had almost made it to safe territory...but he still had two feet in the restroom hallway. *I'm not falling for this bullshit*, he thought.

Margret diverted her eyes beyond the stage. She thought she heard something going on way in the back. Stacey started to stand up. Matt, who was now looking around for Aimee, felt his throat tighten.

Meanwhile, the music was pounding away. Pip had taken the floor on his tenor and sweat was popping out all over him. His playing was fat and expressive. He growled and grunted and was deep in the groove when he heard the commotion behind him.

The timing was all wrong, the vibe was bad, but Aimee wasn't going to be dissuaded. She grabbed Bo's arm and pulled him into her.

It had now officially become an assault. Bo was dumbstruck by her audacity. This was too surreal to imagine.

She was much stronger than he'd guessed. He tried to pull away from her grip and fell back into the wall behind him.

Kim had decided to come to the club and was now watching everything in slow-mo from her chair in the office. Suddenly she shot through the doorway, and very tersely said, "Miss! Do you know how hard it was to get Chanel *and* Stef Dalton here tonight? Do you have any idea?"

Aimee wasn't prepared for the intervention but had come too far to stop now. She mashed her mouth into Bo's who pushed her away. Of all nights! With his wife there, a journalist and somewhere, maybe, a record label scout.

With all her strength, Kim threw her hands on Aimee's shoulders and pulled her back. Jesse had just come into the hallway and quickly inserted himself into the melee, skittering the young woman towards the back exit. "Do you want me to call the police now or wait until you've caught your breath?" he seethed. "Because I'm more than ready to press charges. You dare assault one of my musicians with a whole roomful of witnesses. I'll wait while you decide."

Matt had made his way to the back, followed by Margret. Stacey stayed put to focus on Stef. Fortunately, most of the audience was enjoying the set and continuing to order lots of alcohol. Stef had a second sense that told him to add another song.

Aimee's mascara streaked in all directions across her face. "He put the moves on me!" she screamed. Jesse got her out into the cold night air and then kicked the door closed. "Say it again. I want to hear you lie twice," he said to her.

Matt turned to Bo, pleading, "I know all about this. I'm so sorry. Just let me take her home." Matt knew at that moment he'd have to decide exactly what the next years of his life were going to look like. "Aimee, come with me, now!" he said.

"Wait a sec, my friend," said Jesse, who knew they weren't friends by any definition. "You're not taking her anywhere. I'm about to make a citizen's arrest. Bo, do you want to press charges?"

All kinds of crazy thoughts were swimming in Bo's head. The one that rose to the top was his CD. It was launch night. All the hard work, all the love and pain that preceded it, had brought him to one conclusion.

"Nope," he said. "I'm ready for this psychopath to find another job, and yes, you can quote me." Margret loved this man. "I have music to make and a packed house. Peace out, I've got a bass to play."

CHAPTER 90

The launch date had been a hit. Stef and Shanny were acting pretty cozy together at Bo and Margret's after-party, and both Tim and Pip had brought their significant others. Joey said he had to get home and take care of his dogs. And in the morning, they all got back to their normal lives.

One week after the performance, USA Today ran Stacey Redbone's music review which called the CD "an outstanding, incendiary legacy piece." Aimee was miraculously transferred to an off-site medical office and her replacement was already being trained by Carol.

Bo was still in high spirits. "Lymus would have gotten a kick out of that night, huh? I bet he would have pounded on that piano."

"I think so. I think I heard him," Margret said. "Then you're really okay with things now? Even if you don't get any acknowledgement that he was the original composer?"

"I'll have to be. This is what it is."

She let his words hang in the air for a bit; almost unsure of going forward, but she did. "You know in your heart of hearts – we know – the truth of the matter. Are you disappointed?"

Bo sighed. He looked over at his bride and smiled. "Not really. The CD was my impossible dream, and we made it a reality. I hope people learned a little about Lymus, about the kind of musician he was, and the man he was."

"What next?" she asked.

"There's just one small detail hanging out there. I still have that cease-and-desist from Fetterman, which Zack said is probably nothing."

CHAPTER 91

Bo subscribed to several magazines about jazz and the upright bass. Most were online, but he still liked the physical experience of turning the pages, so he'd bought three subscriptions that were mailed to him. Even between working at the hospital and, lately, finishing the CD, he still made time to finish every issue from cover to cover.

One afternoon Margret left work early to go to the dentist. It took much less time than she planned, so after telling Bobby Slovitz she was calling it a day, she went home. She was going to cook Bo one of his favorite dinners.

It was only a few hours shy of her normal quitting time but it felt luxurious. She snapped on Judge Judy and assembled the ingredients for her Paella **a** la Mags. It was a chicken-based dish with lots of caramelized onions, green peppers, browned chorizo, fresh garlic and extra paprika over saffron rice.

The apartment smelled insane. Judge Judy broke for a commercial. Margret went to tidy up the mail table and saw a recent issue of Jazz Lives. She opened to a spread of an old jazz photograph called "A Great Day in Harlem" which featured no fewer than 57 musicians in front of a row of brownstones around 1958. While the photo was not news per se, she thought it was fascinating that the two authors of the article were able to track down and interview the children or close relatives of all of the musicians. There were other historical photos in the article including one of the slave's quarters from a major US plantation in North Carolina, which was tied into one of the musician's ancestors and the reason, he claimed, that he became a musician himself.

There was no reason that this journey – Bo's hunt to track down the details of his great-great uncle's life, the photos and sheet music from the museum, and the newspaper clippings of Little Dexie Abbott – should stay hidden.

Margret knew that failing to get Lymus a mention in *The Scandals of Violet* bothered Bo. All hope of any such recognition withered away now that Fetterman was trying to flip the story and say, of all things, that Bo ripped *him* off.

Feeling Bo's sense of defeat, she decided to do something about it. She picked through his stack of jazz magazines, searching for a way to bring Lymus out of the shadows and into the current jazz vernacular.

She found what she was looking for in DownBeat Magazine.

CHAPTER 92

Margret reached out to the editor of the magazine and pointed out the coverage they'd received in USA Today, and proposing an article with more in-depth coverage of Lymus's life and Bo's new CD. The magazine was definitely interested. She'd be hearing from one of their writers, they told her.

Four days later – a testament to timely journalism and the significance of the story – the article was posted. It was incredible; more than she'd hoped. Now her only goal was to keep Bo off his computer as much as possible until the print edition came in the mail and she could have it framed.

She put the other musicians and Jesse on notice. They all agreed to keep quiet.

It was tough having such a huge secret, but it would be worth it in the end.

Two days later, she received the magazine in the mail. In person, the article had a life of its own. She was mesmerized by the cover photo which featured Lymus's sheet music inset with an unfocused photo of a tall, smiling young man. The headline read: "A Journey Down to the Roots of Jazz." It ran two and a half pages with numerous other pictures that were attributed to Bo's family, the Civil War Museum at the Smithsonian and the Rayners from Charleston who had donated the sheet music. With the issue in hand, along with the CD and his grandmother's wooden medallion that Bo's cousin reluctantly parted with, she sought out a professional framer to arrange all the items into a shadow box.

She'd put a rush on it.

CHAPTER 93

Three days later, Margret woke up with her stomach twisted in knots. She had picked up the framed piece the day before and hid it overnight. She was so excited about giving it to Bo. He was going to go nuts.

"Hey hon, the alarm just went off. You getting ready?"

"Just a second!" she said brightly.

The present was hidden in a closet, obscured by long winter coats. She was about to get it when she made a quick beeline to the toilet. After she retched into the bowl, she rinsed her mouth. *The stress of this secret has been killing me. Now I can finally tell him!*

"Bo, I have a surprise for you." She carried the present into the bedroom. "Sit on the bed. Don't worry, you won't be late."

"Okay..."

"Now close your eyes."

"It's not my birthday, you know."

"Well no. But it's April and we love April because it's International Jazz Month, right?"

She set the picture on the bed. She'd left it unwrapped. "Open your eyes."

The first thing Bo saw was the sheet music, then the wooden medallion, then the cover of, could it be –

DownBeat Magazine? At first, he didn't understand what he was looking at.

"Babe."

"Yes?"

"You did this?"

"Well, me and a team of writers and editors and photographers, I assume."

Bo put his face into his hands and started crying. Then he pulled Margret to him. "This is unreal. I don't know what to say. How did you even do this?"

"It wasn't easy, and I had to keep you away from your laptop. But all worth it, huh?" she beamed.

"Oh my God. The best present I could ever imagine. You already know what this means to me."

He looked closer at his Gramma's oak medallion, which had haunted his dreams for decades: a bird in flight, trees remote and untouchable, and a stylized sun streaming down its rays. He couldn't believe his cousin had relinquished it.

He hugged her so hard that her chest hurt. "Love you, babe," she said. "Find a good place for it."

CHAPTER 94

After throwing up for three more days without any other symptoms of being sick, Margret decided to take a pregnancy test.

No wonder why her breasts had hurt.

Two small, pink lines on the test stick confirmed her suspicions. They were going to have a baby, and they were both over the moon about it. Bo's mind wondered about how things would change.

"I was thinking about our jobs," he started. This was nerve-wracking territory. Could they even afford child care?

Margret looked over at him. He was going to be a dad. A very handsome, loving dad.

She was peeling potatoes for a homemade shepherd's pie. The crust came from the store but the ingredients were fresh; she even shucked a fistful of pea pods. "We've always said if this happened, I would be the one to go back to work," she said. "Economically it makes sense. You can stay home with the baby and concentrate on your music and teaching online. What do you think?"

Bo came over and gently took the peeler from her hand, rubbing her belly, which was not entirely flat anymore. "Actually, that's perfectly aligned with what I was thinking. I'm blessed to have you for a wife." He kissed her and lingered, then came in for another, less hurried, kiss.

"Which is it, buddy? Shepherd's pie or shimmy over to the bedroom?"

They were both hungry and now Margret was eating for two. Bo shelved his mood.

"Okay, so say this weekend we start to crunch numbers," he said. "By the way, the podcast I did last week turned into some great press. The video got about five thousand views so far. A blogger from Italy wrote about the CD, and we also sold a few hundred more singles on Apple and Amazon."

"Nice going! I hope this CD blows the doors off," she said. "Between that, your online lessons and not paying for childcare, we might do okay."

This new journey together was worthy of a song. Bo came up with a few chords and popped them into his composing software before they left him.

Raylin Rose would know the difference between a *da capo* and a *coda*, and between *pronto* and *pianissimo*; she'd know how to swing, bop, drag and double-up. She'd know how to construct a melody and how to deconstruct a time signature. Bo would make sure of all of that.

Life would change for them in unimaginable ways. There'd be fights and hormones, financial freak-outs and bone-deep exhaustion. Neither had any idea how the other would parent, but like a song with a smart melody and a good rhythm, it had all the fundamentals.

Bo snuggled up to Margret and dropped to her belly, singing Gramma's song – Lymus's song – to the baby. Had his great-great uncle been around, he would have seen proof that the notes he wrote on a fragile fabric were not forgotten.

CHAPTER 95

The email had a "Fetterman" address in those solid capital letters, evoking the same terror as the earlier messages. And now the next in line, Bruce Fetterman, would have his say.

Dear Bo,

I need to speak to you about my father and the Cease and Desist letter his lawyer sent. Please call me as soon as possible. I didn't have your telephone number or I would have called you myself.

Bruce Adam Jason Fetterman

Bo rubbed his temples. Another Fetterman headache. *I don't have two cents for them to go after. And now a baby on the way. What the hell do they want from me now?*

Bo knew this needed to be dealt with immediately. He called Zack. "Find out if he'll do a Zoom call with both of us," Zack said. "I doubt he'll agree to it but it's worth a shot. We need to put the kibosh on this situation."

When Bo emailed back and proposed a Zoom call with his attorney present, Bruce surprisingly agreed. Zack was giving up his family time on this precious weekend. He had toddler twin boys, and his wife bundled them up to go to the zoo. Zack shot her an imploring look and promised her the call would be quick, which he didn't know for a fact. She unzipped the kids and plopped them on the couch.

They dialed in and saw that Bruce Fetterman was a large man who bellowed when he spoke. His email icon was a photo of Dizzy Gillespie. Maybe that was a good sign?

Zack started things off. "Mr. Fetterman—"

"Please. I call you Zack, you call me Bruce. Go on."

So far, so good.

"Bruce," said Zack. "Bo brought me up to speed with your father's letter, or rather his lawyer's letter, the C&D. What can we do for you?"

Bruce wheezed and dipped off-camera for a minute to hack up a lung. "Sorry about that. Too many cigarettes at intermission."

"No problem." Bo could think of a hundred better ways to spend a Sunday afternoon, but this had to be resolved. Whatever "this" was.

"Zack." Bruce let his voice resonate. "Plain and simple: my father is 92 and quite frankly, he's losing his mind. His faculties."

Zack waited a beat. He knew a lot about pacing a conversation. "I'm so sorry to hear that."

Bo added, "Me as well."

Bruce continued. "Not only does he mean no harm, neither does his damned lawyer, who'll do anything my father asks. I don't want to waste your time, gentlemen.

Bernard Fetterman has no case, no grounds and no grudge against you, Bo."

Bo looked at Zack who lowered his lids and turned his head slightly to one side to indicate not to say anything yet.

Zack asked the million-dollar question: "What is this really all about, then?"

Another phlegmy outburst. "My mother put a bug in his ear. She may be paranoid, but she's not losing her faculties. She was there when he opened the video announcing your CD, and she went bonkers."

Bo had a hunch about sending him the video. Margret was right. He shouldn't have.

Bruce continued. "She leaned over to my father and said *that's the young bassist who was at the Met. Why is he playing 'My Heart has Feathers' without your permission?* I know she said this because I was at their house in Miami Beach preparing a brief. I'm an eminent domain attorney."

"What was your father's answer?" Bo asked.

Bruce smiled or winced. It was hard to tell. "He said, and this I quote, 'That untalented bastard ripped me off, and he's gonna pay, and I'm the one who's going to sue the pants off him.' I asked him what he meant because I'd just walked into the room, so he played it again. I nearly hit the floor.

"I know this music very well," Bruce continued. "I know the original Elsner and Price opera, and I know the music from *The Scandals of Violet* intimately. If you say that the melody of your song is from your slave ancestor – is it okay to call him that? – objectively I would have to admit there's more than a similarity. I would venture to say," here he took a deep breath, "that it only makes sense, date-wise, that your relative's melody came first."

Had they both heard correctly? Bo sat stunned, frozen in place. Zack could read his expression and, though he was just as shocked, tried not to slam the table or break into cartwheels. Bruce had just stated there was more than a coincidental similarity between Lymus's song and the *Scandals* theme song. The music actually matched, and Bruce acknowledged that Lymus's had to come first. Where to go now?

Zack maintained his composure and spoke up before Bo could react. "I'm very happy to hear you say that. Then I guess the C&D is null and void?"

Bruce seemed not to notice their stone-like expressions. "Yes. It's a product of Mom's paranoia and Dad's vengefulness and quite frankly, his losing touch with reality. I don't know how he could have heard that music, but there is no mistaking the melody. I was a music theory minor during my undergrad and I'm a bit of a jazz buff myself."

Bo was about to speak. Zack held his hand up and smiled. "And what about the fact that, as you say, the music seems to be the same. Can we have that in writing?"

Now it was Bruce's turn to stiffen up. "I mean, I shouldn't have said that. But I did. Don't get too excited, though, since any pertinent statutes have long since passed, making it legally inconsequential. Still, I'm prepared to get this behind us. I'm the Power of Attorney for my dad, so I'll put it on family letterhead: The C&D is no longer in force, and there are *strong similitudes* between the two songs, without saying which is derivative. Will that work?"

Wish granted. Allow the man to save face. Bo knew there was no way to get compensation for his family line, and though a Playbill addendum wasn't on the table, an admission of this caliber signed by Bernard Fetterman's son would be the Hope Diamond. He quashed his emotions. Margret was not going to believe this.

"Yes, it will work," Zack said evenly. He couldn't believe his ears. He was trying not to explode on camera.

"Alrighty then. And I'm sorry to waste your time and that my father stirred the pot unnecessarily with his lawyer's threats. As a huge jazz fan, Bo, you have a new follower." Bruce folded his hands in front of him. He was sitting very close to his laptop camera and almost filled the screen.

Bruce continued. "I'll send this to you by email attachment and then I'm gonna give that schmuck lawyer the back of my hand for indulging Dad's every irrational impulse. But there is one more thing."

Bo already knew silence was golden. He waited. He had gotten all that he wanted and more.

"Unfortunately, I've missed your release day performance," Bruce said. "Your vocalist, Chanel, was tremendous in the video. To have seen her live would have been more than thrilling."

Did the Fettermans want to steal her from her record label?

Bruce blushed. He looked like a totally different person. "I want an intro to Chanel. Please."

Oh, so that's what this was all about. The big guy didn't give a rat's patootie about his father or Lymus's song. He only wanted some female companionship. Doable, thought Bo, but only if she agreed. Men were not her favorite species lately.

"I think I have her whole discography." Bruce wheezed and cackled at the same time, which didn't seem anatomically possible. "I love her earlier R&B work and I've been infatuated with her for about five years. I'm divorced, so there's nothing untoward."

"Of course not," said Bo, who was straining for the conversation to be over. "I'll get back to you on that by tomorrow. I should definitely be able to get you a phone call," God willing, he thought, "but as far as a personal meeting, I'll have to check. I need to respect her wishes."

The big man loosened his tie. Why was he dressed up on a Sunday? "That sounds groovy. I appreciate it. Look for that letter in your email tomorrow. Really sorry for the hassle, man."

Trying to be hip with a bass player: comedic. Getting everything that you've asked for: priceless.

CHAPTER 96

Bo walked into his music room and sat on the loveseat, looking at the framed piece Margret gave him. "Lymus, you devil," he said aloud. "Your genes have been passed down for over 100 years and still your music won't be denied. I wish you could be here today to listen to the CD. I think you'd really like it."

At his core, Bo had always felt the magnetism between rhythm and harmony, mood and melody, pace and purpose. With these artifacts of the past that had come home and were now displayed on his wall, Bo had honored his ancestor in a small way.

The setting sun at half-past-six insinuated its last bits of orange light between the blinds. Bo studied the geometrics of the final glints of light coming through. Don't stare at the sun; don't fly too close.

Turning his back to the window, Bo was struck by seeing how the sunlight had sprayed itself onto the opposite wall. Black lines of shadow from the slats were striped with deep gold hues from the setting sun and reminded him that life was only light, air, space and reflection.

OUTRO (Epilogue)

Tim McKnight paid the bills by selling backing beats to jazz musicians and filmmakers. When he added hip-hop to his repertoire, he became a millionaire. He bought a small home in the garden section of Brooklyn's Manhattan Beach, two blocks from the water, and he and his husband learned to paddleboard.

Pip Jones and Elisa Solloway (now Jones) moved to the artsy community of Cotuit on Cape Cod. He founded a jazz guild and opened a tiny storefront that sold graphic T-shirts and lick-proof sunscreen for hairless dogs that Elisa invented.

Joey Fritz perfected the weighted drumstick and got an angel investor, who dropped the deal when he showed up at her home in his pajamas. He never played jazz again.

Bruce Jason Fetterman had a few dinner dates with Chanel before she ghosted him. He quit smoking, discovered CrossFit and became a regular at karaoke bars, favoring the songs of Steven Sondheim.

Chanel's career took off like a rocket and she became a household name. She fell in love with Bruce Fetterman but never told him, not wanting to impose the demands of a celebrity lifestyle on him.

Jesse and Kim Hendroff expanded The Minor Seventh after it was named number six of the 10 Best

Jazz Clubs in New York City. Kim quit smoking and her cancer remained in remission. Her hair came back full force in pure silver.

Bernard Fetterman passed away at the ripe age of 97. On his deathbed, he divulged the truth about the *Scandals of Violet* song to Lottie, his wife of 64 years, saying he had heard it somewhere before, though he forgot where. She forgave him for lying and kissed his forehead.

Stef Dalton's career retrospective CD went platinum shortly before his health took a bad turn. Chanel flew in from Los Angeles to visit him in a nursing home and held his hand for the last time.

Aimee Janeth Patel left her new job at the medical office and took a cab to Newark International Airport where she started her life over in Ft. Lauderdale. She joined a repertory theater company and enjoyed playing male leads "just to get inside their heads."

Matt Singelli was heartbroken after Aimee left him until the next semester, when he met an adorable freshman who volunteered to edit his new book about the Fertile Crescent.

Zack Adams started his own law firm. He and his wife had another set of twins; this time, girls.

Margret Sonski-Abbott decided she loved marketing after all, just not in healthcare. She found work at a foster home and fell in love with a baby boy from Syria, bringing the number of children in the household to two.

Beauregard Sonski-Abbott embraced the life of a stay-at-home dad. He was booked day and night with online lessons and started writing film scores that Tim McKnight pitched to all the right people.

Raylin Rose Sonski-Abbott (RayRay for short) wrote her first symphony when she was eleven. She was the youngest student ever accepted to Julliard. On her first day there, she showed her father's CD to the Music Theory professor, who used it to teach the entire course.

ACKNOWLEDGMENTS

Since starting my jazz blog in 2016, I've cultivated an endless posse of brilliant musicians to bounce ideas off, and this book has been no exception. Thanks to the many who have been excited about the story and encouraged me along the way. In particular: I'd like to thank bassist Mark Wade; author Gary Rosen (*Jazz Age Lawyer*); my self-publishing mentor and the smooth jazz artist Maurice Johnson; life-saving editor Calen Nakash; soprano sax innovator Sam Newsome; Dave Ratner (Creative Law Network); Mathilde Mukantabana (Ambassador, Embassy of the Republic of Rwanda) and David Canady (photographer). Thanks also to my loving and ridiculously dependable support network. You are precious beyond infinity: Vicky, Rachel and Tim, and my one and only love, Richie.

Debbie Burke is an award-winner editor, ghostwriter and the author of *Tasty Jazz Jams for Our Times*™ *(Vol. 1 and Vol. 2), Glissando – A Story of Love, Lust and Jazz, The Poconos in B Flat* and *Music in the Scriptures.* Her jazz blog at debbieburkeauthor.com has earned international praise, and she is the founder of Queen Esther Publishing LLC, a professional editing and author coaching firm.

Brooklyn-born, she has lived in six different states in the eastern half of the US but most of all loves being near the ocean. When she isn't writing, she's learning new licks on the sax.

Follow the author on Amazon at

bit.ly/DebbieBurkeAuthor

(case sensitive)

and please consider leaving a review.